THE
PRICE GUIDE
TO THE
OCCULT

THE
PRICE GUIDE
TO THE
OCCULT

LESLYE WALTON

CANDLEWICK PRESS

Copyright © 2018 by Leslye Walton

First edition 2018

Library of Congress Catalog Card Number pending
ISBN 978-0-7636-9110-3

17 18 19 20 21 22 LSC 10 9 8 7 6 5 4 3 2 1

Printed in Crawfordsville, IN, U.S.A.

This book was typeset in Adobe Jenson Pro.

Candlewick Press
99 Dover Street
Somerville, Massachusetts 02144

visit us at www.candlewick.com

To my parents.

Time and again, I thought there was only darkness left in the world.

Time and again, they showed me there was still light as well.

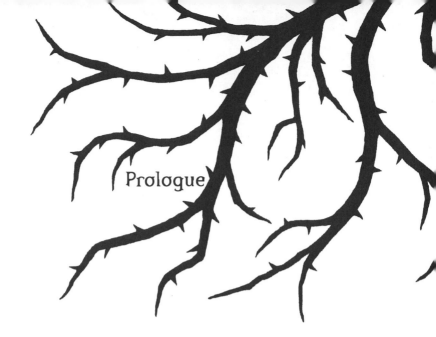

Prologue

They have been called many things.

Years ago, when their nomadic ways led them north to where the mountains were covered in ice and the winter nights were long, the villagers called to them, "Häxa, Häxa!" and left gifts of lutfisk and thick elk skins. When they moved farther south, they were Sangoma and as honored as the village's own traditional healers. In the east, they were the fearsome Daayan; in the west, they were called La Lechuza and were rumored to have the ability to transform into birds. They've been called healers and seers, shape-shifters and conjurers. Wise ones. Heretics. Witches. They've been welcomed and revered as often as they've been feared and despised. History books throughout the world are filled with tales of their spilled blood — blood spilled willingly or unwillingly.

A family by the name of Blackburn was known to be particularly talented. Their talents delved deep into the realms of intrigue — clairvoyance, telekinesis, divination. They used their gifts to heal the sick or to ease the passing of those they could not heal. They used their gifts to help build towns or to defend them. Some of them were lovers, some of them fighters; a fair few were both. For centuries, over lifetimes, the truth of their power seemed everlasting, a blooming flower that would never wilt, a full moon that refused to wane. That is, until Rona Blackburn made the fateful decision to move to an obscure island off the Washington coastline and brought that long line of impressive family talent to a rather catastrophic and unexpected end.

Anathema Island sits at the tail end of the San Juan archipelago that winds through the cold waters of the Salish Sea. The word *anathema* refers to something dedicated to the gods. Coincidentally enough, it can also indicate someone accursed, someone damned, someone doomed. A fitting name, it would seem then, for an island buffeted by rain-bearing winds and cloaked in a sky so gray that the ocean and the heavens seemed one and the same. It was a place so remote and so inconsequential that cartographers rarely bothered to mark it on maps.

The island's absence from atlases didn't matter to the

swell of Lhaq'temish families who'd inhabited it for centuries. But that flourishing community fled and scattered throughout the archipelago like leaves in the wind with the arrival of eight daring settlers, who never bothered to ask if the land already belonged to anyone else.

Mack Forgette, having failed to find his fortune in the gold mines of Canada's caribou country, was the first of the eight to arrive, in 1843. Soon after came Jebidiah Finch, an experienced farrier. The man they all called Port Master Sweeney had been a trapper. It was his keen eyes that kept watch over the small dock on the southwest corner of the island. Forsythe Stone, an evangelical pastor, imagined leading his fellow islanders away from the debauchery and immorality that tend to infect men left to their own devices. Avery Sterling was a talented carpenter. Simon Mercer came from a long line of farmers. Otto Birch, the good German, migrated from a small town in northern California. And they all considered themselves quite lucky with the arrival of Doctor Sebastian Farce, his black medical bag, and his opium ampoules.

Each man claimed his own piece of land — a few hundred acres on which he kept goats and sheep — and built a small shack where he slept with his boots on. A meal was a piece of hard cheese or jerky carved with the same knife used to dig out splinters and ingrown toenails. They shat outdoors alongside the goats.

It would be another few years before their wives and

children would join them. And so, it was in this way that the menfolk of Anathema Island lived. Until one blustery day, at the cusp of yet another long, hard winter, they received a rather unexpected and uninvited guest.

"She was alone you say?" Jebidiah Finch asked.

Port Master Sweeney nodded. "If you don't count the two dogs, if you can call them that. They were some six hands tall, like mythological monsters. But they were nothing compared to her. I've never seen a woman so large. She towered well over my head. At first, I thought one of you unlucky bastards might have ordered himself a bride, but it seems the woman is here on her own." The port master shuddered then, remembering the other unmistakable feature of this giantess: one glass eye that twisted angrily in its socket. The glass eye a shade of violet not found anywhere in nature.

"Perhaps the lady is a witch," Otto Birch suggested.

The other men laughed, but the port master did not join them.

"Yes, tell us, man," said Mack Forgette. "Where might we find this heretic?"

"I am pleased to say that I do not know" was Sweeney's stoic response.

Avery Sterling turned to Sebastian Farce, who until then had been sitting in quiet contemplation. "What do you make of this, Doctor?"

"She may be an unusual woman," the good doctor said after a moment, "but she is still a woman. How much trouble can she cause that we men would not be more than able to counter?"

"I do not think it wise to underestimate her," the port master said, still shaken. "Mark my words, Rona Blackburn will prove to be a violent and capricious windstorm. God willing, she has no aim of staying!"

Oh, but Rona Blackburn most certainly did.

Rona soon picked out her own plot of land — one hundred eighty acres that stretched along the bottom of a rocky hill and only a stone's throw from the shoreline. Quickly, much more quickly than natural for a man much less a woman — even one of Rona Blackburn's stature — a house appeared. She filled her new home with reminders of her previous one on the Aegean island she had loved so much: pastel seashells and a front door painted a deep cobalt blue — a color the yiayias always claimed had the power to repel evil. Then she set up her bed, made a pit for her fire, and erected two wooden tables. One table she kept bare. The other she covered in tinctures and glass jars of cut herbs and other fermented bits of flora and fauna. On this table, she kept a marble mortar and pestle, the leather sheath in which she wrapped her knives, and copper bowls — some for mixing dry ingredients, some for liquid, and a few small enough to bring to the mouth for sipping. And when the fire was stoked and the table was set, she placed a wooden sign — soon covered in a blanket of a late December snow — outside that blue front door.

It read one word: *Witch*.

For all the things people have said about Rona — and they've said many things — no one could ever say she lacked a sense of humor.

Throughout that first long winter, and well into the following summer, the Original Eight steered clear of Rona Blackburn. They did not lend a hand or make any other offering, of friendship or otherwise.

Rona built a fence and raised a small barn. She purchased a few chickens and goats from a reclusive family whose presence on the other side of the island the others had failed to notice. She found a beehive in the woods and moved it closer to her house. When spring finally arrived and the bees awoke, Rona harvested the most succulent honey. She planted a garden that exploded in a profusion of sunflowers, zinnias, dahlias, lavender, rosemary, hyssop, thyme, and sage. In the hot summer months, there were carrots, cucumbers, beans, and tomatoes the size and shape of small boulders.

And all the while, the Original Eight kept their distance.

And then.

The eight were felling trees to build a steeple for their church. As per Forsythe Stone's instructions, the steeple would be tall — tall enough to be seen from every part of the island, a holy arrow that would point the godless and faithful alike toward righteousness and glory.

The leather strap used to drag the felled trees up the hill weakened and snapped, sending an avalanche of logs back down the hill and clipping Sebastian Farce on the way.

No one remembered who suggested bringing the doctor to Rona. Perhaps it was Sebastian himself, though by the time they reached Rona's door, Sebastian had stopped making much noise at all.

Rona must have known that saving one of them could be the path to either acceptance or repudiation. For centuries, Blackburn women had been run off for perceived offenses less serious than causing someone's death. Nonetheless, Rona stepped aside and allowed the men to carry the injured doctor through her cobalt-blue door. Once the patient was settled, she sent them on their way.

Blackburn women had never been much for an audience.

With Sebastian's blood still sticky on their clothing, the men turned and headed back to their shacks. Some of them were gravely quiet. Others were wide-eyed and chatty, the adrenaline compelling them to recount the disaster time and again.

Sebastian Farce awoke the next morning, his wounds miraculously sealed, and his blood pumping, as it should, through his veins and not onto the floor.

For the next two days, Rona tended the doctor's wounds while he read from her treasured volumes of Greek myths, her two dogs curled up at his feet. In the evenings, under a sky full of stars, they passed a rosewood pipe and discussed their shared avocation. He spoke of his leather tourniquets and opium tincture. Rona told him about magicked stitching and countless herbs. At night, they sealed their affair with whispered oaths and christened the bedsheets with sweat.

And then, just three days after the accident, Sebastian Farce reminded himself of his marital vows, of the wife and three children he'd call for in a few months' time. Telling himself that Rona was nothing more than a brief moral blunder, he snuck out the back door of Rona's cedar house, skirted the sleeping beasts in the yard, and walked home with the shame of his actions tucked between his legs.

Eventually he told the rest of the men of his misdeed, and they all laughed nervously and easily forgave what they decided was a blameless indiscretion.

"You were beguiled," said Simon Mercer.

"Undoubtedly the victim of some kind of black magic," agreed Otto Birch.

"She must have muttered an incantation over your sickbed," Mack Forgette offered, "or slipped a tincture down your throat."

"My God, man, how else could you explain yourself," the port master exclaimed. "To bed a woman such as that? A woman such as *her*? It was a temporary madness to be sure!"

Thankful that they had evaded the eyes of the witch, the

other seven men chose to forget that she had saved one of their lives and hoped she would find her way off the island, if not immediately, then certainly before the arrival of their wives and children.

Sebastian Farce could not forget as readily. He became consumed with darker thoughts.

Unable to sleep at night, Sebastian's mind began to wander. If Rona had the ability to bewitch him, to use her charms and enchantments to heal him, didn't it follow that she could just as easily use black magic to harm him? His wife? His children?

Rona was thinking no such things. But she could feel Sebastian Farce's paranoid thoughts creeping into her mind like an invasive weed. In a short time, this man — whom she had kept warm in her own bed, had fed with food prepared with her own hands, and had baptized with the sweat of her own body — began to fantasize about finding her floating facedown in the lake. Rona was aghast at how quickly his fear and guilt had curdled into hatred and contempt.

The summer droned on, with its long hot days and even hotter nights. Autumn came, painting the island trees with its golden hues. In late October, they awoke to winter's first dusting of snow. And then, exactly one year after Rona had first arrived on the island, Sebastian Farce decided to take matters into his own hands.

"If we are to purge the island of her," he said to his brothers in arms, "we must do so now, before she pollutes

9

the minds of our wives and our daughters. And before our sons fall prey to the wiles of the witch."

They came carrying firearms and torches, ignorance and fear. Their fear rained down on Rona's burning house like ash. It blinded them to how the flames merely licked her side, like the rough tongue of a wild cat. They didn't see how easily she strode out the back door with her beasts at her side, how their bullets pierced her skin and then melted, leaving a torrent of liquid lead in her wake. They didn't see how she stood hidden in the trees, a dark shadow against the night, the hounds beside her growling like low rumbles of distant thunder. Cradling the swell of her growing belly hidden under her skirts, Rona watched the Original Eight burn her home to the ground.

Later, drunk on whiskey and the exhilaration of the hunt, the men sifted through the remnants of Rona's home; they found nothing but a hypnotic purple glass eye, staring up at them through the ashes. They brazenly mounted that eye on the wall of the Willowbark General Store alongside the rest of their trophies — stuffed pheasants and wild turkeys and the head of a black-tailed deer. Forsythe Stone, the evangelical pastor, likened it to staring into the eye of a storm. He claimed it proved them heroic. In truth, it was further evidence that the Original Eight were simply a bunch of damn fools.

Rona returned in the dead of night, waking them with a piercing scream that chilled their blood and shattered their eardrums. She banished the darkness with a blinding light that they later swore radiated from her fingertips. And she brought with her something far more terrifying than fire: an army of wooden leviathans, hybrid monsters carved from trees, so tall they blocked the moon. The foolish men could only watch, blood spilling from their ears, as Rona's monsters tore down their homes. Even they had to admit it was fair reparation: an eye, as they say, for an eye.

But for Rona, simple retribution wasn't enough. She knew how much they wanted her to disappear from the island, how much they wanted all trace of her to vanish as cleanly as the tide erases footprints in the sand.

So, when Rona felt that familiar urge to leave, to carry on with the nomadic ways of every witch that came before her, she searched for a spell that could silence the call in her blood. Rona wanted Anathema's animals to thrive on the oxygen from her lungs. She wanted to carve out the island's landscape with her own hands and for its rivers to flow with the sweat from her own brow.

Her search for such a spell led her to the branches of the Blackburn family tree. She traced limbs that reached to the heavens and bent back to the earth again. She followed roots that stretched across all parts of the world and were inscribed in languages that had been dead for centuries. And there, buried deep beneath those gnarled roots of that ancient family tree, Rona found one.

She cast a binding spell and etched its words into her

own skin, strengthening it with the potency of her own spilled blood. Using the sharp blade of her knife, she also carved the name *Sebastian Farce* into the parts of her he had blessed with his mouth: her hips and thighs, the curve of her neck, and the swell of her breasts.

When her daughter was born, Rona picked up the knife and pricked the bottom of her infant's foot. Their mingled blood spread like an ink stain across the mattress, and Rona crooned that spell once more, this time as sweetly as a lullaby.

A binding spell requires one to peel back the layers of her soul and stitch them to another entity entirely, such that she is no longer herself, but a chimera made of her own flesh and blood and *something else*. It is black magic, wicked and terrible, and as Rona learned all too well, black magic always comes at a wicked and terrible price.

Rona's daughter Hester possessed none of her mother's natural talents for magic. Until she was nine years old, that is. At that age, she could suddenly run faster than any man — or boy — on the island. Hester became the fastest sharpshooter west of the Rockies. Many claimed that it was the threat of a gun clenched in her small hands that kept a single drop of blood from being shed during the Pig War between the United States and the British Empire — as long as you didn't count the poor pig. But Hester's gift for speed was both the start and the end of her abilities.

Starting with Hester, no Blackburn woman ever again possessed the full range of her ancestors' gifts, gifts that should have been her birthright. Instead, the gifts were splintered and parsed — each generation benefitting from only one. Should this splintering of talents have been the only unintended side effect of Rona's binding spell, perhaps the Blackburn daughters could have been content. But sometime in her nineteenth year, Hester awoke to find she could think of only Andreas Birch, the son of the good German, to the exclusion of all else. Just as suddenly, Andreas was similarly afflicted. For three days, the two were consumed with exploring all of the ways their bodies fit together. On the morning of the fourth day, Hester awoke alone. She later found Andreas back behind the grocery counter. His face, red with shame, was the only evidence of their passionate affair until the second Blackburn daughter, Greta, was born nine months later.

A Blackburn woman's love story only ever lasts three days. When it is over, the man returns to his life, to his children and his wife if he has them, never once acknowledging — often times, not even to himself — the part he played in the creation of another Blackburn daughter.

Rona wanted to expunge the names of those foolish men from all of history. She did not expect that by doing so, she'd inadvertently tied their bloodlines, one by one, to her own until it was Blackburn blood that had the greater claim on Anathema Island. In casting her vindictive spell Rona unwittingly damned every future Blackburn daughter to heartbreak and a loveless union.

For seven generations, the fates of the Blackburn daughters have been bound to Anathema Island and to the descendants of the Original Eight. One can't help but wonder what this might mean for Nor, the eighth and therefore last of the Blackburn daughters. Could it be that for her, love was a choice, a hand she could either grasp or push away? And, more importantly, would that impressive line of family talent finally come to a quiet and unremarkable end with her?

Nor had been counting on it.

Cloaking Spell

"Everyone longs to go unseen once in a while.
The trick is not to find oneself trapped in invisibility."
— Rona Blackburn

Nor Blackburn wasn't afraid of blood.

There were several things she was afraid of, but blood wasn't one of them. This was fortunate, because when she picked up shards of glass from the cup she had dropped, she cut her finger, and it bled. It bled a lot.

For a moment too long, Nor looked at her finger and watched the blood well up and trickle into the sink. It reminded her of how, in the past, she had sometimes been "careless" with knives when loading the dishwasher or chopping vegetables for dinner. It was a way to cause pain without appearing to do so deliberately. It was a way to disguise spilled blood as accidental.

Nor ran cold water over her finger and then wrapped it quickly with gauze. She was more careful when picking up the rest of the broken glass. Nor wasn't afraid of blood, but not being afraid of blood was one of the things she *was* afraid of.

In her bedroom, Nor found the little dog still asleep on her pillow and an early morning September rainstorm beating against the windows. She stretched her arms over her head, and her fingertips brushed the slope of one of the eight walls that made up the room. With windows and a skylight on every side, Nor's room seemed closer to the heavens than to the ground. At night, the dark blue of the sky was her blanket, and the glow from the stars illuminated her dreams. On clear days, she could usually see most of the island from up there. On this morning, a thick, dreary fog blanketed the ground, and Nor could see only the tops of the trees along the shoreline and the rocky gray waters of the Salish Sea.

It had been Nor's great-grandmother, Astrid — a woman who could lift a length of timber twice her size over her head — who had built the Tower in the shape of an octagon, making it virtually indestructible. "It is not impossible to destroy a witch," Astrid had been known to say, "so her home should be sturdy enough to at least give her time to escape through the back door."

Nor pulled a pair of ripped jeans out from under a pile of clothes on the floor. She tugged the jeans up over her hips and pulled on a black sweater. The stretched-out sleeves flapped at her sides like broken wings, but they did a good job covering the thin white scars that ran across her wrists and along her upper arms.

She paused just long enough in front of the mirror to line her blue eyes in shimmery black and attempt to rake her fingers through her wild waist-long hair. She found her phone on her dresser beside an old book of Greek myths, then snagged her muddy running shoes by the laces and stepped over her grandmother's dog, Antiquity. The wolf-hound, transfixed by a pair of crows perched outside one of the windows, gave a low growl.

"Oh, hush," Nor scoffed. "We both know you'd have no idea what to do with one if you caught it. Your hunting days ended lifetimes ago."

Antiquity pondered the truth behind this, then, giving a final huff at the crows, stood, pushed past Nor, and bounded down the stairs, the windows of the house rattling with each thunderous step. The little dog in the bed burrowed farther under the covers.

Unlike the rest of the Blackburn daughters, Nor's gift — or "Burden," as the Blackburn women called it — hadn't arrived until the first penumbral lunar eclipse after her eleventh birthday. She had awoken early that morning — so early that the moon still shone brightly in the dark February sky — to find her grandmother Judd standing at the end of her bed.

"Well, what is it then?" Judd had spoken around the

rosewood pipe clenched in her teeth. Having only moved into the Tower the year before, Nor had been still unaccustomed to her grandmother's gruff ways. Her heart had quickened when Judd peered at her; there was never any hiding from her all-seeing eyes.

Judd was the sixth daughter, Burdened with the gift of healing. Nor had always feared those times when she found herself at her grandmother's mercy, when all of her discrepancies, all of her flaws and fears were exposed, and Judd calmly repaired the parts of her that she'd broken.

"Take a deep breath," Nor's grandmother had ordered. Nor did as she was told, and a surge of relief filled her. She felt — nothing. Perhaps she'd been spared? Judd exhaled a plume of smoke so that the next breath Nor took was thick with it. It tickled her throat. And in noticing that, she'd noticed something else.

"I can hear the bees," Nor had whispered, and, closing her eyes, the sound of the hibernating hive in the garden grew louder in her head. "They aren't talking to me exactly. But I can hear them. I can hear their queen. The next snow will be here in a week. And the rooster in the yard will be dead by spring."

Judd confirmed Nor's Burden with a firm nod. "So the plants and animals can talk to ya, can they? That's a fine one, Nor."

Nor had understood what her grandmother was telling

her then: that she was safe. As long as Nor stayed content with her innocuous ability, there was little chance of her becoming like her mother.

Which was why, long after Judd had gone back to bed, eleven-year-old Nor had watched the moon fade into the morning sky and tried to pretend that the Burden she'd told her grandmother about was the only one she'd received.

Although a fair portion of Anathema Island remained mostly uninhabited, the more populated part of the island was a composite of farmhouses and beach rentals, historic buildings and the occasional tourist trap. Most of the shops and businesses sat along the main road, Meandering Lane, named for the way the street twisted and turned along the island's southwestern coastline.

The Witching Hour sat atop the Sweet and Savory Bakery. As Nor started up the outside stairs, she noticed the door to the bakery had been flung open, and the aroma of freshly baked bread — cinnamon and pumpernickel and sourdough — wafted over her. She could see Bliss Sweeney, a smudge of flour on each of her rosy cheeks, sharing a morning cup of coffee with Vitória Oliveira, the proprietor of the Milk and Honey Spa down the street. They both waved when they saw Nor.

"Would you mind putting these out for your customers?" Nor asked. She stopped and handed each woman a stack of flyers she pulled out of her bag. "I promised they'd be on every countertop of every business on the street."

"Madge is going all out this Halloween, isn't she?" Bliss mused, examining the flyer.

"A lantern-lit midnight tour of the island cemetery. A séance and palm reading. Any chance she'll convince our own young Blackburn to join the festivities this year?"

"Not if I can help it," Nor said with a smile.

"But what if Rona Blackburn shows this year?" Vitória Oliveira teased. "Madge has been making that promise for years."

"All the more reason for me to stay at home," Nor said. "I'm going to turn out the lights and eat all of the candy Apothia buys for trick-or-treaters."

Bliss laughed. "No interest in meeting your infamous matriarch?"

"Not in the least."

Despite her being a Blackburn, no one on Anathema had ever treated Nor any differently from anyone else. Eclectic characters were just a part of island life. This, after all, was a place where street names were reminiscent of fairy tales, with names like Red Poppy Road and Stars-in-Their-Eyes Lane. It was a place where bohemians came to retire, to spend their free hours creating sculptures out of recycled electronics or painting large graphic nudes of one another that they proudly displayed at the weekly street fair. It was where Harper Forgette — who, genealogically speaking, was

Nor's sixth cousin — and her girlfriend, Kaleema, ran an alpaca farm on the Forgette family land. It was where clients looked forward to a taste of Vitória Oliveira's lavender jam just as much as they did to her lavender-infused pedicures, and where Theo Dawson, the island's sole mechanic, had been known to accept payment in croque monsieurs.

Heckel Abernathy, the owner of Willowbark General Store, on the other hand, insisted to all who would listen that the Blackburn family was very special indeed. To him, they were the living embodiment of a good luck charm or a talisman, and the cause of the island's good fortune. It was understandable why he might think so. The link between the Blackburn daughters and the island was so strong Nor often imagined that the veins that ran underneath her skin and the tree roots that ran under her feet were one and the same.

The island itself was rich with relics of Blackburn family lore. A plaque sat in front of every building constructed by Astrid Blackburn, the fifth daughter, designating it a historical landmark. A statue of Astrid's mother, Scarlet, stood in front of the library she'd rescued books from when a fire surged through the island in 1928. The island cemetery boasted headstones of all five departed Blackburn daughters, as well as Rona Blackburn herself. It was said that leaving a white lily on the grave of Mara, the third daughter, would ensure safe passage into the afterlife for departed loved ones.

And though there were many stories about why these

extraordinarily gifted women could do the extraordinarily gifted things they did, thankfully for Nor, those who truly believed it was because they were *witches* were few and far between.

Nor left the bakery and continued up the staircase, careful not to slip on the wet blanket of red and orange leaves covering the steps. The second-floor porch had been decorated for the season with cornstalks and pots of Chinese-lantern flowers. A hand-painted sign in the window read:

GUIDED WALKING TOURS OF ANATHEMA ISLAND'S

WITCH-RELEVANT LANDMARKS AND LEGENDS.

AVAILABLE THRICE DAILY.

FOR TIMES AND PRICES, INQUIRE WITHIN.

Nor stomped her wet boots, entered the shop, and was greeted by the tiny clang of bells and a thick haze of incense. Walking into the Witching Hour always felt to Nor like she was walking into a secret. The dark purple walls and velvet curtains gave the room an air of mystery. A black-painted pentacle covered the wooden floor. Short, fat candles flickered from the windowsills. Grimacing gargoyles and death masks hung from the walls alongside dried herbs and shelves of apothecary bottles filled with all kinds of nefarious contents: graveyard dirt, dried scorpions, bat's blood. There were broomsticks that smelled faintly of cinnamon, and tall, pointed hats crafted by a local milliner. The shop even had its own familiar, a skittish black feline by the name of Kikimora.

It was a shame really. If any of the Blackburn daughters had been gifted with a talent for spell work, the Witching Hour would have had everything they could ever need. But the art of casting spells had died with Rona, it seemed. *And good riddance to it,* Nor thought.

As Nor hung up her jacket, a woman she'd only ever known as Wintersweet bounced into the room, a black-hooded cloak hanging from her shoulders.

"Tonic?" she squeaked, offering Nor a mug. "Just brewed it this morning."

Nor took the mug, trying to avoid the woman's gaze as she waited, expectantly, for Nor to take a sip. When she did, Wintersweet clapped her hands gleefully and skipped back into the adjoining room. Nor put the mug down. The contents tasted too vile for her to drink.

Nor took her place behind the cash register as the participants of the morning's tour began to trickle steadily into the small shop, rain jackets and umbrellas dripping. The Witching Hour's owner, Madge Shimizu, appeared in the back doorway.

"You forgot this," Madge teased Nor, then plopped a tall, black, pointed hat onto Nor's head. Nor grimaced, and Madge laughed. "If you get a chance," Madge said, "there are some boxes in the back that need to be stocked." She pulled up the hood of her own black cloak and welcomed the small crowd. Once she and Wintersweet had led the group out into the rain, Nor plucked the hat from her head and tossed it to the floor.

Despite the best efforts of a well-meaning guidance counselor, Nor had dropped out of high school after her junior year. In their last required meeting, the counselor had declared that Nor lacked, to use her words, "the intrinsic motivation to do anything of importance or relevance with this life."

This wasn't exactly a surprising revelation. Teachers had been saying roughly the same thing about Nor for as long as she could remember. Nor's report cards were typically littered with phrases like "lacks initiative" and "is easily discouraged." She did, at her grandmother's insistence, take the exams required to earn her General Education Diploma — which, it turned out, wasn't actually a diploma, but a certificate that Nor was supposed to print off the Internet herself.

Nor had never had the heart to tell anyone that all she wanted was to make the slightest mark as humanly possible on the world; she was too preoccupied with proving to herself that she was nothing like her mother to be focused on anything else. Which was exactly why the link to that GED certificate was sitting unopened in Nor's inbox, and she was still working the same delightfully dull part-time job at the Witching Hour, stocking the shop's sagging shelves with tarot cards and spell kits, selling faux love potions to tourists, and attempting to stay awake through slow afternoons.

Nor had unpacked half of the new merchandise, restocked the apothecary section with mandrake root and sumac berry, and added a fresh pile of the Witching Hour bumper stickers — *I'd Rather Be Riding My Broom* — to the front counter by the time Savvy entered the shop a few hours later. She was carrying two tall blended coffees from the Sweet and Savory Bakery, which Nor eyed greedily.

Savvy, Nor's best friend, was a petite beam of sunshine in scuffed-up combat boots and ripped lace leggings. A punk rock Pollyanna, she was sweet and genuine and, in Nor's opinion, extremely pretty with big brown eyes, ocher-brown skin, and wildly colored hair.

"So how was school?" Nor teased, gratefully taking the coffee.

Nor didn't envy the load of books she could see in Savvy's hot-pink backpack or the hours of homework she'd have to complete this weekend.

"Nothing but a shell of its former self since you left," Savvy said. "They say no one in the history of the school made a greater impact there than you did."

"Must have been all those clubs I didn't join and all the classes I cut."

"The dances you didn't attend, the yearbook photos you never took." Savvy shook her head. "I've never known anyone so devoted to anonymity."

"Have I told you I don't have a single social media account?"

"Ugh, don't remind me." Savvy stood on her tiptoes to swipe at the handwoven dream catchers hanging from the ceiling. "I tried messaging you about tonight before I remembered the only way to communicate with you is through carrier pigeon."

"Or, you know, you could have texted me."

"Semantics."

"What's happening tonight?" Nor asked. She felt something brush against her leg. She looked down. Kikimora meowed at her silently until Nor picked her up and placed her on the counter.

"A bunch of us are thinking about heading over to Halcyon Island," Savvy said.

Some of the islands in the archipelago were so small that they were privately owned. Halcyon was one such island, named for the wealthy family who had purchased it in the 1940s. The novelty of owning an island in the Salish Sea was lost on the Halcyon heirs, and Halcyon Island was later sold. It had exchanged hands multiple times: the most recent owners — a pair of well-meaning mainlanders — had converted the Halcyon family mansion into a bed-and-breakfast. It had closed a few years ago, and the island had been empty ever since.

Nor made a face. "I don't get why you like hanging out there. It gives me the creeps."

"I thought we liked things that give us the creeps?" Savvy said.

"We do," Nor said. "Just not that place. They found a body over there, Savvy."

"It's not there anymore!" Savvy retorted. "Plus, we live on an island. What the fuck else is there to do?"

"You could go to work," Nor suggested jokingly. "Isn't the Society supposed to be open now?"

For years, the barn behind Theo Dawson's mechanic shop had been where islanders brought belongings they no longer needed or wanted. Though money never exchanged hands — the Society for the Protection of Discarded Things, as Savvy fondly called it, was more a take-what-you-need-and-leave-the-rest kind of place — Savvy still spent most of her free time behind the front counter. She was, to use her words, the Guardian of Unwanted Things.

"I could do a great many things, but that doesn't mean I will" was Savvy's reply.

Nor laughed and nudged Kikimora out of the way before she lifted another heavy box onto the counter. Most of the books and curios that Madge ordered for the shop came from places with names like Crystal Waves and the Enlightened Sorcerer. Nor found a publishing house called Crone Books particularly irritating because its logo was the silhouette of a stereotypical witch, complete with a long, pointed nose and a wart on her chin.

This particular box, however, was unmarked. The return

address was from some obscure town in Maine that Nor had never even heard of. She ripped the box open. Savvy reached in and pulled out a book from the stack inside.

"*The Price Guide to the Occult*," she read aloud. "Intriguing title." She flipped the book over. "*A collection of magick spells, passed down for generations and now available for common use for the first time ever.* They even spell *magick* with a *k*."

"If that doesn't make it legit, I don't know what does," Nor said sardonically. In most of those so-called spell books, the spells typically read more like recipes, most of which, for reasons Nor had never been able to understand, required the person who cast them to be naked under a full moon. She doubted very much that this spell book was any different.

"Wait," Savvy said, flipping through the pages. "It's not actually a spell book."

"What is it then?"

"It's exactly what it says it is. A price guide. A catalog, like the kind they put out for tulip bulbs every spring. You send in your order form and your money, and then I guess they cast the spell for you."

"That's generous of them."

"Isn't it? Because apparently magick-with-a-k is far easier to perform when someone is willing to pay for it."

"Well, it is the American way."

"Yup. There's a free one in the front that you can cast yourself. Claims to help with memory. What do you think? Feeling forgetful today?" Savvy's smile dropped. "Oh wait, it says, 'non-practitioners of conjuration'—it really does say that—must perform a blood sacrifice first.' What a load of crap."

"Let me see that." Nor pulled the book from Savvy's grasp. She read the advertised spell, absentmindedly fiddling with the bandage on her finger.

It was a spell. A *real* spell.

As a child, Nor had spent every winter solstice, full moon, and spring equinox with Madge and the rest of her coven of wannabe witches. They would gather in the clearing near Celestial Lake to sing songs and dance around a bonfire with flowers in their hair, chanting "spells": meaningless words strung together with the intention of rhyming more than casting magic.

But this spell was nothing like that. This was a Blackburn spell, the kind only Rona herself could cast. *How in the hell did it end up here?* Nor opened the book. And that was when she saw her face: those piercing green eyes; that provocative stare; the fingernails filed to a point and painted with scarlet lacquer; matching red lips; a complexion so pale her skin appeared to be made of porcelain. Her hair was different, now a shiny orange-red cut in the style of a 1940s starlet. All cheekbones and coy. After all this time, there she was again.

An onslaught of memories filled Nor's head. *The night sky bright with fire. The charred black of burned skin. Pools of blood.* The scars on Nor's arms and wrists began to hum in anticipation. Her fingers tingled with want for something sharp.

"What is it?" Savvy asked, her voice wavering with concern. "Nor, what's wrong?"

The thump of Nor's frantic heart was so loud she didn't hear Madge coming up behind them until it was too late. Madge grabbed the book from Nor and stared at the photo. Then, clutching the book to her chest, Madge let out a strangled moan, as if a part of her had shriveled and withered away.

"It's my mother," Nor whispered.

2

Tranquility Spell

"A wish for a tranquil mind is a wish for an apathetic one."
— Rona Blackburn

Nor's run after work that day took her far into the interior of the island, around Celestial Lake, past the waterfall, and up into the cliffs that edged the island's western shore. She paused there, wiping the sweat from her face and catching her breath while she admired the view. Nor never grew tired of it. All choppy gray water and gray skies and no one but an occasional breaching humpback whale as far as the eye could see.

Two tiny sparrows hopped along the branch of a nearby pine tree, fluffing up their feathers in the rain and chirping at each other fondly. Animals, Nor had learned, have their own names for each other. Best translated, they were typically things like Winsome, Persnickety, and Sanctimonious. Of these two, one called himself Vigilant, the other Balderdash.

Out in the water, a pod of orcas moved gracefully through the waves. She could just make out the black splotches of their dorsal fins through the drizzling rain. Their thoughts were content and peaceful, and Nor could feel the quiet of the world below the surface wash over her. She closed her eyes, and she was there with them, gliding through those cold waters. Ribbons of sea kelp anchored to the ocean floor brushed against her belly. Tiny fish darted in and out of view. Nor opened her eyes and sighed.

To Rona and her forebears, being able to communicate with nature had meant being able to sway the movement of the tides; to bring rain to parched lands; and to come to the aid of the whales in the sea, the birds in the sky, and the beasts on the land. On her best days, Nor could sometimes predict the weather. It was nothing compared to what her grandmother could do, and Nor had done all she could to keep it that way. She had as much interest in manipulating a passing rainstorm as she did in trying to control the ever-changing color of Savvy's hair.

She liked the simplicity of this Burden. She liked knowing that rose bushes could fall in love and that leaves sang as they fell, a lilting sigh synchronous with their slow descent to the ground. Most trees could dream as well; all Nor had to do was observe a forest at dusk to know it was true.

The leaves' autumn song accompanied Nor as she took the long way home, choosing the trail that curved around the lake instead of Meandering Lane. The rain had stopped, and the air felt cold and crisp in her lungs. Her arms pumping at her sides, Nor tried to push out the image of Madge that kept playing in her head. It scared Nor to think of how she'd wilted to the floor as soon as that book was in her grasp, suddenly transforming into the faded, fragile shell that Fern had left behind years ago. What could her mother accomplish with a multitude of fans like Madge at her service? Fans willing and able to do just about anything to keep Fern happy?

When Nor reached the lake, she paused to stretch and was surprised to find she wasn't alone. A little ways off the beaten path, she saw a boy with dark hair attempting to skip rocks across the water. With each failed attempt, he grew more and more sullen. He was short — probably a good two or three inches shorter than Nor — but compact and sturdy. With a sinking feeling, she recognized him. It was Gage Coldwater.

The Coldwater family mostly kept to themselves, though Nor had always felt a certain animosity directed at her — specifically from Gage, who'd been in her grade at school. Savvy claimed she was paranoid, but Savvy hadn't witnessed the fit Gage Coldwater had pitched in seventh grade when he and Nor had been paired for a science project. He'd even stormed out of the room — and received a week's detention for it — when the teacher refused to reassign partners. It had been humiliating, to say the least.

The Coldwaters supposedly lived up here, though exactly where and for how long, Nor had no idea. All she'd ever seen were hemlock trees and snowberry bushes and black-tailed deer skirting around the trail; she'd never seen so much as a single house, let alone several.

Gage wasn't alone. A girl with the same dark hair sat beside him on the wet ground. She was chewing her lip, lost in serious contemplation. The girl had what looked like tarot cards spread out on a black cloth in front of her. When it came to tarot, Nor was no expert, but she was impressed; if she didn't know any better, she would have thought the girl actually knew what she was doing.

"You know the ground's wet, right?" Gage said to the girl. He lodged another rock at the lake. It landed with a lively plop. He scowled.

The girl — *Charlie*, Nor thought, suddenly remembering Gage's cousin's name — looked up at him and rolled her eyes. "No shit," she said. "Just shut up for a minute. I'm trying to figure something out."

"Can you imagine what Dauphine would do to you if she found out what you're doing?" he snorted. Charlie jumped up and punched him hard in the arm. "Come on. You know I would never tell her!" he said, wincing. "That woman already has it out for us."

"She has it out for *you*," Charlie said, sitting down again. "She likes me. She just thinks I keep bad company." She looked at Gage. "Any idea who that might be?"

"Not a clue." He picked up another rock and tossed it into the lake. "You could have at least waited for the sun to come out."

The girl peered at the spread in front of her. "No, I couldn't," she said. "I need to do this now and I'm struggling with how to interpret this reading. You know that body they found on Halcyon Island last week?"

"What about it?"

"I don't know. Something about it just seems . . . strange."

Gage leaned over her shoulder and pretended to study the cards. "I don't know if this is helpful, but I'm pretty sure this card means that you're full of shit." He laughed. "Come on. It's an abandoned island in the middle of nowhere! They probably thought, hey, here's my chance to die in peace. What's so strange about that? I actually envy that person right now."

Charlie ignored him. She looked at the book she had open in her lap and then back down at the cards. "That it's an abandoned island in the middle of nowhere is exactly my point. I have this feeling that —" She stopped midsentence, closed the book with a snap, and swept her hand across the cards to scramble them. She'd spotted Nor, and soon after, so did Gage.

"What the hell are *you* doing here?" Gage asked, glaring at her. Charlie rushed to gather up her things, then wrapped the black cloth around the deck. As she hurried past Nor, she didn't notice one of her cards flutter to the wet ground.

Ignoring the sour look Gage was giving her, Nor picked up the card. On it was a picture of two people falling from a tower atop a rocky cliff. There was a lightning bolt in the sky and flames shooting from the tower windows. It gave Nor an unsettled feeling. Charlie took it from her, and the two left without another word. Nor finished her run wondering what it was Charlie Coldwater thought she had seen in those cards.

Nor cut across Red Poppy Road and hopped the fence into the fields where Harper and Kaleema let their alpacas out to pasture. Alpacas hummed when happy, a cheery ascending noise that sounded a bit like a kazoo, and it was a herd of buzzing alpacas that was soon escorting Nor the rest of the way home. The Blackburn home loomed ahead, a dark shadow against a fading sky. It was as imposing as a fortress. Much like her grandmother.

Nor tried to imagine the best way to tell Judd about her mother's reappearance, about her book. She should probably tell her right away. *Just get straight to the point*, as Judd was always telling her. As if speaking with a woman known as the Giantess was ever easy.

I'll find a way to tell Apothia instead, Nor decided. Nor's grandmother and her partner, Apothia, had been together since before Nor was born. Better to let Apothia figure out how to tell Judd than her. Because what would she say? Her mother was doing the unthinkable and selling spells that hadn't been cast for generations — spells for success, good luck, beauty, revenge.

Like an ancient relic from the Old World, Rona's spells and the diary she'd recorded them in were kept only for their sentimental value, as a link between themselves and their matriarch, a reminder of times that once were and never would be again. From what Nor had been told, the last Blackburn daughter capable of casting spells was Rona herself.

The dogs met Nor at the fence. Antiquity flung her giant front paws over the top of the gate and cast a disparaging look at Nor through a thick gray forelock. The little dog poked his nose at her through the lower slats of the fence. Quite the contrast of the larger dog, Bijou, as he called himself, was a happy little thing who always dreamed of sunshine and fireplaces. It made sense. Antiquity had been alive for going on nine generations now, but Bijou could still be considered a puppy and was about as ordinary as they came. Not that Nor would ever suggest such a thing.

Nor coaxed Antiquity down from the gate and followed the two dogs onto a path of river rocks that led to the Tower. In the light of the setting sun, the stones glowed like the embers of a dying bonfire.

The path spanned the length of the few acres of Rona's original one hundred and eighty that they still held in the

Blackburn name and connected the Tower with the little white dance studio that sat at the very edge of the property.

Visiting Apothia in her studio had been a favorite pastime of Nor's as a small child. She'd browsed through closets filled with traditional silk cheongsams and several tutus, salvaged from Apothia's days dancing with the San Francisco Ballet. Some afternoons, they had sat together on the porch in wicker chairs too frail to withstand Judd's size and drank tea from a tea set hand-painted with cherry blossoms too delicate for Judd's rough grasp. For hours, Nor would ramble on in the way that neglected children do, soaking up all the attention and eating countless tiny chocolates wrapped in brightly colored wrappings until she was so full of both she could burst.

Once inside the Tower, Nor found a kettle sitting in the kitchen's great copper sink, water spilling over the sides. She turned off the faucet, careful not to look at the blank space on the wall over the sink.

A large assortment of knives — all different sizes for different purposes — had once hung there. Each knife was so sharp you could slice your hand without feeling a thing. The only proof of injury would have been the red blossom blooming fast in your palm. It had been over a year since Apothia had locked up the knives. Though Nor insisted the precaution was no longer necessary, locked up was where they remained.

Apothia was exactly where Nor had thought she'd find her, leaning over a wok on the stove, the heat from the steam creating a rosy glow in her papery cheeks. With her short gray hair styled into a puffy pompadour, it was hard to accept that Apothia Wu was almost seventy years old. She still had the poise of the dancer she had been years ago; Nor almost expected to look down and see a pair of pointe shoes on her feet.

Nor took a peek inside the wok and breathed in the aroma of a bubbling hot pot. Judging by the amount of red and green chilies and Szechuan peppercorns amid the tofu and ginger on the cutting board, it was going to be a spicy one. Nor's eyes watered just thinking about it.

Apothia swatted Nor away from the stove. "You shouldn't have gone running in this rainstorm," Apothia scolded her. "You look pale."

"You always say that," Nor murmured. It could be ninety degrees outside and Apothia would still claim that Nor looked pale, as if it were Nor's fault that she had a complexion that stubbornly remained a light fawn color even in the middle of the summer.

Nor's great-grandmother Astrid had constructed the Tower around the remains of Rona's original cedar house, which meant as Nor passed through the kitchen, her feet padded along the same places Rona's once had. Nor imagined she could still hear her great skirts sweeping the floors as she walked. She wouldn't have been surprised if, on turning her head, she found herself staring into that eerie violet glass eye.

Judd sat at the dining room table with Antiquity now curled at her colossal feet. She had her back turned to Nor, and for a moment, Nor watched the smoke from her rosewood pipe wind its wispy way up toward the ceiling and then fade away entirely.

Though Judd was a healer, one didn't ask Judd to cure a broken heart or a bout of winter malaise; her specialty was physical pain. Some pain did not want to be healed; it had to be convinced, compelled, coerced into submission. Some pain gathered on Judd's hands, clinging to her fingers like sticky threads of spiderweb silk. Some pain was drawn out as shards of ice that shattered when removed. Some pain was made of heavy, dense pebbles that filled Judd's massive hands; still other pain blistered her palms, with red seeping wounds that Apothia covered with bandages and thick salve. It was a grueling Burden. And though it was true that few people knew *how* Judd healed, for those she helped, it was simply enough that she did.

Like most everyone who had come into contact with the Giantess, Nor loved and feared her grandmother. She was mountainous and intimidating, but there was a kindness in her scowl, a gentleness in those large hands.

Judd turned, and the chair beneath her groaned. Her long silver hair, loosely plaited, was wrapped around her head like a crown. It was the work of Apothia's quick fingers; Judd's were much too large for such deftness and too damaged, mangled by thick scar tissue running from thumb to forefinger, the result of so many healings. Tonight those hands were holding a copy of Fern's book, *The Price Guide to the Occult*. Judd tossed the book onto the table with a loud smack as Nor sank into the chair across from her.

"When did you find out?" Nor asked.

"Just today," Apothia answered for Judd, coming in to set a little cast-iron pot in front of Nor. She furiously rubbed Nor's wet and unruly hair with a towel until Nor swatted her away.

"Eat something," Apothia ordered before disappearing back into the kitchen.

Nor took the tiniest bite of tofu and bean sprouts before she pushed the bowl away and picked up the book. She recognized spells in Fern's book as their family spells — each and every one with a price attached to it. There was the Weather Jinx, the Spell of Misfortune, Fire Scrying, and the Hex of Guilt, known to bring about hallucinations thanks to a helpful handful of those deceitfully pretty belladonna blooms. But there were other enchantments listed in Fern's guide that Nor didn't recognize. Something called Void of Reason claimed to grant the power of mind control, and the Revulsion Curse was supposed to suppress your appetite.

Nor closed the book. She'd been counting on the fact that the art of incantations and spell work had disappeared with Rona Blackburn upon her death in 1907. But looking at them here, Nor was suddenly beginning to have her doubts that that was true. Dread filled her stomach. Her mind filled with images she'd rather forget. *The charred black of burned skin. Pools of blood.* "What's going to happen if she can actually cast these?" she heard herself ask.

"Nothing good, that's for damn sure," Judd replied, peering out at Nor behind a haze of smoke. "She'd have to commit some pretty terrible acts to perform magic that's got nothing to do with her own Burden. And something just as terrible is bound to happen because of it."

She was right. For Fern to practice magic outside her naturally bestowed Burden would require a sacrifice, the kind that caused great anguish. The kind of pain that Nor knew her mother would inflict on another without hesitation. It was likely she would find it quite entertaining, amusing even.

Nor nervously ran her fingers along the inside of her arm; even through the fabric, she could feel the thin keloids of scars there. "So what the hell do we do?" she muttered.

"Not too much to do, girlie," Judd answered. "Not right this second at least." She stood, shoved her feet into a pair of giant-size boots, and reached for her rain jacket. Antiquity pulled herself slowly from the floor, shaking the stiffness out of her arthritic joints. "Especially since I promised Harper Forgette I'd see what I could do about that cough of hers tonight."

42

The Giantess and the wolfhound disappeared into the darkened yard. Nor flipped on the light switch beside the door. Behind her, she could hear the sounds of running water and Apothia humming to herself quietly in the kitchen.

Nor stared out at the trees, now illuminated by the triangle of light pouring from the porch light. Silently, she counted the lines of raised scars that marred her wrists and the crook of her elbows. She counted them until her hair no longer hung wet from the rain, until she no longer felt like she was choking on the pounding heart lodged in her throat.

It took a force of nature to drive pain away. And as Nor finally turned away from the door, she reminded herself that, while she may not have been such a force, her grandmother most definitely was.

3

Transformation Spell

"One should make a point to master even the most basic
transformation spell. At some point in time, everyone yearns
for the ability to change into someone else."
— Rona Blackburn

The next morning the grass was wet and gleaming. The
remains of yesterday's rain shower dripped steadily from the
pine needles. Bijou followed Nor down Meandering Lane
but stopped just beyond the humming alpacas basking in
the morning sunshine. It was a beautiful day, the sky a lapis
lazuli blue, the leaves — dashes of red and gold and brown
drifting across the pavement — the only sign that it was
September, not April or March.

Along the side of the road were white yarrow, thistles,
and a resilient geranium peeking out from beneath the
gnarled root of a tree. Blue lupines swayed gently in the

breeze. A few weeks ago, Kaleema had planted daffodil bulbs in the garden beds in front of their farmhouse. Come spring, the yard would be a mélange of yellows.

When Nor was young, she used to pretend daffodils were teacups. She'd have tea parties in the garden in front of the Witching Hour; Madge had once helped her stretch the quilt from her bed out across the dirt, and Nor had spent the day serving dandelion heads and handfuls of clover on the maple leaves she used as plates. Later, Madge had brought out cookies and sugary-sweet lemonade. While Nor had eaten, Madge had pulled her into her lap and woven garlands for Nor to wear in her hair.

It was one of the few happy moments Nor remembered from her childhood. She had no such memories of her mother. With Fern, kindness turned to malice far too quickly for it to be trusted. Causing people pain was a game to Fern, and Nor was often forced to play. It was a game Nor never won.

When Nor turned the corner, she found that the end of Meandering Lane had been transformed, as it was every other Saturday morning. The road, closed to any traffic, was a scattering of pop-up tents and folding tables. The usual locals and tourists ambled through the street. Mothers and fathers pushed small children in strollers as older siblings followed on bicycles. A young couple shared a cup of hot chocolate and cookies, warm and gooey, wrapped in crinkly white paper.

Eclectic pieces of installation art and handcrafted pottery were on display in front of the Artist Co-Op. Outside Theo's mechanic shop, a collection of sea glass in shades of blue — azure and cerulean, cobalt and beryl — had been spread across a woven blanket.

"What do you mean, what're they *for?*" Savvy scolded some poor passerby. "They're *pretty!*" Savvy's hair today was a sunset of hot pink and fiery orange, piled on top of her head in a mess of natural corkscrew curls.

Harper Forgette and Kaleema peddled their scarves and sweaters of alpaca wool beside Reuben Finch with his artichokes, rainbow chard, and parsnips, all of a size that surely only he could grow. Catriona, one of Nor's former classmates, was selling smoked salmon and cedar grilling planks alongside her gentle — and equally pleasantly plump — mother. It wasn't like they had ever been friends, really, and it seemed rather pointless to start pretending now, but Catriona waved, and Nor waved back.

As Nor climbed the stairs to the Witching Hour, she passed by the bakery, where she could see Bliss Sweeney, her hands deep in a billowy ball of dough, talking animatedly with a customer. A line a few people deep zigzagged its way out the door.

Nor was holding her breath when she walked inside the little shop, but whatever she was expecting, it wasn't there. A few tourists perused bins of healing crystals; others awaited

Vega, the on-site palm reader, to tell them their fortune. A group of chatty older women awaited this morning's guided walking tour. Fern Blackburn's book was prominently displayed by the cash register, but it didn't seem to be garnering much attention. In fact, it didn't look like they'd sold many copies at all.

Though her mother had been gone for years, there had never been a time when Nor hadn't feared — even expected — her return. It had always seemed inevitable, a recurrent nightmare that leaked into her dreams. Even on the brightest of days, the dread of Fern's return was a black smudge on the window, blocking out the light.

Perhaps her fears were unwarranted; perhaps her mother's charismatic hold over people wasn't quite as strong as Nor feared it might be. Or maybe she'd changed, transformed into someone benevolent and kind. Maybe they'd be lucky this time? But as soon as Nor allowed that thought to comfort her, she remembered this — no one in the Blackburn family had ever been considered lucky.

By late afternoon, the farmers' market had been disassembled. The last whale-watching tour of the day had returned hours ago, and though Savvy had popped in a while back, Nor had quickly lost her to the tented space Vega used to conduct his readings.

In an attempt to keep herself from falling asleep behind

the counter, Nor started to unpack a box of incense onto a nearby shelf. The names of these things had always amused her: Citrus Linen, Fresh Waterfall Mist, Heaven.

Who in the hell has to decide what heaven smells like? she thought. *I would hate that job.*

The sound of clanging bells drew Nor's attention to the door. Madge entered the shop, followed by a handful of tourists, all buzzing with excitement from the afternoon tour. Nor held her breath, but most of them were more excited about purchasing a breakup spell kit or protection charm than her mother's book.

Madge lowered the hood of her cloak. Wisps of her glossy straight black hair were stuck to her flushed cheeks. Nor searched Madge's face for any sign of yesterday's distress but thankfully saw none.

"Think you could pop over to the Milk and Honey Spa and pick up some essential oils for me?" she said to Nor. "Otherwise, Vega's evening readings will be sans aromatherapy."

"That would be quite the travesty."

"Mock if you must, but most people find having their fortunes read very comforting," Madge insisted. "You of all people might benefit from letting him take a look at yours."

"Fat chance of that happening," Nor said, "but don't let that stop you from trying."

"You know I won't." Madge tugged on Nor's wild

48

hair fondly, and though Nor rolled her eyes, she smiled nonetheless.

"Just make me a list of what you need," Nor told Madge. "I'd hate to get ylang-ylang when what you really need is sandalwood."

"Now that *would* be a travesty," Madge agreed. She handed Nor a quickly jotted list as well as a stack of flyers for Nor to leave on the spa's counter. As she did, Savvy emerged from Vega's tent looking suspiciously delighted by something.

Madge seems to be back to her old self. Even Savvy and that exasperating look on her face are about as normal as it gets, Nor thought, feeling relieved.

"So tell me," Nor asked Savvy as the two traipsed toward the Milk and Honey Spa.

"Tell you what?" Savvy asked, feigning innocence.

"Don't give me that. What did Vega say? Are you going to unexpectedly receive a large sum of money? Meet a tall and handsome stranger in a darkened alley?"

"Okay, first of all," Savvy said, "if I meet any kind of stranger in a dark alley, I'm going straight for their tender parts. I don't care how handsome they might be. Second, Vega said I am going to face an unexpected challenge, if you must know." She absentmindedly tugged at the silver hoop in her left eyebrow. "And that it's important I make a good impression this week."

"A good impression on who? No one new or interesting ever comes here." She caught a dirty look from a tourist walking by, and Nor leaned in closer to Savvy. "You know Vega's predictions never really have anything to do with *you* specifically, right?" she said. "He's probably told that fortune to ten other people today."

"Well, if you're suddenly such the expert fortune teller," Savvy teased, offering Nor her outstretched palm, "you give it a try."

Nor stared at Savvy's hand. The last Blackburn daughter capable of palmistry was predictably Rona Blackburn. The closest anyone else had ever gotten was Greta, the second daughter, who had been given the heavy Burden of prophetic dreams. To the rest of the Blackburn daughters, foresight of any kind — reading tea leaves, palms, runes, or tarot cards — might as well have been a foreign language. To Nor, palmistry was just another piece of Rona Blackburn's legacy in which she had no interest. She shook her head and looked up at Savvy, who was still grinning at her expectantly. "Just looks like a bunch of lines and squiggles to me."

"But you've spent your whole life in Madge's shop," Savvy said cajolingly. "And you're a *Blackburn*. Some of it must have rubbed off on you." She hadn't moved her hand. "Come on. Throw some of that old black magic my way."

Out of the corner of her eye, Nor saw the lines in Savvy's palm begin to glow and flash. She tried not to notice the obvious break in Savvy's heart line, quickly shut her eyes, and willed away the jumble of unbidden words that filled her head.

"I guess it doesn't matter," Savvy said. "But you're wrong about no one coming to the island. I saw Reed Oliveira on my way back from school on the ferry last week."

Nor's eyes flew open, her pulse jumping like an electric spark. "But he — he left," she stammered. "No one ever comes *back* to Anathema once they leave."

Savvy shrugged. "Yeah, well, no one ever moves here, either, do they?" she said. She gave Nor a knowing look, and before Nor could think of a valid excuse to turn around, Savvy was dragging her down the street toward the Milk and Honey Spa, Reed Oliveira, and Nor's certain humiliation.

On an island as small as Anathema, the arrival of new neighbors could cause quite a stir, especially when those new neighbors included two teenage boys like Reed and Grayson Oliveira. The first time Nor had seen Reed was also, incidentally, the first time Nor had attended the high school located on one of the larger islands. Though school had never been something at which Nor excelled, she'd allowed herself a brief moment of excitement as she walked down Meandering Lane, and she had even stopped at the Willowbark General Store before the forty-five-minute ferry ride to school.

One of the first structures ever built on the island, Willowbark was a small gray one-room building that sat alongside the ferry dock, and though the building had been rebuilt after the great fire, the original store sign still hung above the front door. The island was full of homegrown gardens of different varieties, and most households made their own bread and churned their own ice cream, butter, and cheese. Some harvested honey.

But Willowbark was the only place on the island that sold any kind of nonperishable item — laundry detergent, shampoo, boxed macaroni and cheese, and name-brand peanut butter. Willowbark was where the kids on the island bought king-size candy bars, cinnamon rolls delivered fresh from the Sweet and Savory Bakery, and cups of hot chocolate with mounds of chocolate whipped cream to sip on the ferry ride to school.

On that morning, the store's few aisles had been filled with roaming bleary-eyed kids, the same ones Nor had gone to school with all her life, and all with their opinions about her: two pretty cheerleader types who'd never given someone like Nor a second thought, and, at the cash register, Catriona, who wasn't nearly as pretty or as popular as she wanted to be. A few kids from the Coldwater family had been there as well. As usual, Nor made a point of avoiding Gage.

She'd ducked quietly out of the store, self-consciously tugging at the fingerless gloves Apothia had knit to cover the bandages on her wrists. They were wool and itched almost as much as the scabs underneath them. Nor had been silently lamenting Savvy's proclivity for tardiness when she saw him: a strange new creature standing out on their little dock like some kind of miracle or myth.

Leaning against one of the railings, his long body propped up by sinewy muscled forearms, Reed Oliveira had given the impression that he couldn't care less about being the new kid. But Nor had spent enough of her life attempting to draw as little attention to herself as possible, and she had become an expert observer by default.

Nor had heard that Reed's dad had died suddenly just a few days after moving to Anathema Island. Losing a father was something with which Nor could empathize. She missed her father so much, just thinking about him could often bring tears to her eyes. Of course, the big difference between Nor and Reed was that Nor had never actually met her father. What would it be like, she'd wondered, to actually have a father, and then to lose him? She'd imagined that loss would be unbearable.

So, to her, Reed Oliveira had looked sad. Afraid. Most of all, he had looked lost, like a boat that had suddenly become untethered. Nor had known exactly what that felt like.

Nor still hadn't spoken to Reed by the end of that first quarter. Not on the ferry on the way to school or when she'd passed him in the hallway. Her French class was the period directly after his, and sometimes they'd passed through the doorway at the same exact time, but Nor was just as invisible to him as to everyone else. And why shouldn't she have been? She had made a point of being unnoticeable, hadn't she?

And then.

It had been raining all week, a gray, blustery kind of miserable, and that morning was no exception. It was the day before winter break, and as was an unofficial tradition, most students had stayed home. The few who hadn't skipped school boarded the ferry as usual.

Nor had headed straight for the concession stand, tempted by the scent of freshly brewed coffee. The line was already long, and as Nor had waited for her turn to order, she had tugged her thick scarf tighter around her neck and blown on her fingers in an attempt to warm them. Outside, the rain pounded against the windows as the ferry rocked across the churning water.

It was only when she finally got to the cash register that Nor had realized she was a couple of dollars short. Her face red, she'd mumbled an apology to the barista while hopelessly scouring the bottom of her bag for loose change. That was when Reed Oliveira had tapped her on the shoulder and said, "Let me get that for you."

Afterward, Reed and Nor had carried their coffee cups to an empty table near the back.

"I didn't think you knew who I was," Nor had admitted.

"It would be difficult not to know who you were," Reed had said with a smile.

"I guess it is a pretty small high school," Nor had said.

"And I think your French class is right after mine," Reed had added. "But even if neither of those things were true, I'm pretty sure I'd still figure out a way to get to know you, Nor Blackburn."

Later that night, Nor had been surprised to find a slip of paper tucked into her bag. It read:

Tu es si belle, ça me ferait mal à chercher ailleurs.

You are so beautiful, it hurts to look elsewhere.

It had taken her a long time to write a response. She'd checked her translation over and over again to make sure she'd done it correctly. But when it had come time to give it to him, she'd panicked. All she could think about were the wool fingerless gloves she wore to hide the bandages on her wrists, or how she sometimes lost her train of thought in Mrs. Castillo's class because her plants were always complaining that she overwatered them. If he knew her — *really* knew her — how could she be sure he'd still like what he saw? She couldn't. So she'd torn it up and never brought up the first note with him, either.

Historically, Blackburn love stories lasted three days. Nor's had lasted less than twenty-four hours.

Understandably, Reed had never spoken to her again after that. The following year, Nor had dropped out of school, and then, just like everyone else, he'd left the island shortly after graduation.

And now — now he was back?

"What am I supposed to do with that?" Nor muttered to herself quietly.

As she and Savvy approached the Milk and Honey Spa, Nor could hear the gentle *ping* of cascading water from the tiered water fountain. The sweet perfume of lavender hung in the air. There was basil and rosemary and mint as well — an entire garden sat beside the spa, full of carefully tended herbs and flowers Vitória Oliveira used for her essential oils.

The tranquil ambience continued inside with bamboo wood floors, warm sconce lighting, and soft harp music. On the front desk sat a menu of spa services, everything from mineral mud wraps to deep tissue massage.

Savvy jumped up to sit on the counter. "Yoo-hoo!" she called, swinging her legs and knocking her platform shoes rhythmically against the glass.

"Yoo-hoo, yourself," a voice replied.

And there he was. He'd always been tall, but he seemed leaner — as if he'd lost part of himself while he was away. His dark-brown hair, long and disheveled, hung past his ears, and he had a large silhouette of a bird — a crow, maybe — tattooed on the inside of his tawny right forearm. The rich brown color of his eyes was the same as Nor remembered, as was the twinge of sadness behind that confident, easy smile of his. The way Nor could feel the nearness of him in her pulse — that was the same as well.

"You know no one ever willingly comes back to this place once they escape, right?" Savvy teased.

"I'm just breaking all the rules, I guess," he said, smiling. He motioned toward the flyers Nor held clenched in her hands. "I've never gone to one of Madge's infamous séances. Am I missing out?"

"Nor makes a point of boycotting it every year," Savvy answered. "It's her birthday, you know. October thirty-first."

"Is it?" Reed smiled at Nor, and she could feel her face growing hot under his gaze.

"Madge asked me to pick up some essential oils," Nor blurted out. She thrust Madge's list in Reed's direction.

"We're particularly interested in those dealing with love. Attraction. Seduction," Savvy added.

"Need some help in that area, do you?" Reed said.

"Some of us still have to finish our senior year and are too focused to be distracted by the pangs of love." She sighed dramatically. "There'll be time for that later."

"Whatever you say." He smiled, making Nor's pulse jump again, and held up Madge's list. "I'll be right back with these."

Nor breathed an audible sigh of relief before realizing that Savvy was staring at her, amused. "What?" she hissed.

Savvy smiled. "You're blushing."

Oh, damn. "Am I?" she asked, feigning sudden interest in peeling the dark-blue chipped nail polish from her thumbnail.

"Please tell me you two were secret lovers, and you had a special spot near the waterfall where you would meet every night," Savvy whispered excitedly.

"What? No! People don't do that."

"People totally do that," Savvy interjected. "*I* will do that."

"I'm sure you will. But it was nothing like that. He just—" Nor paused. "He called me beautiful once." She cringed and waited for the laughter.

"Oh, my God, Nor," Savvy breathed.

Nor's blush deepened. "It's not that big of a deal."

"But it *is*. Oh, my God, it *so* is. Maybe you aren't going to die without ever having been in love. I've been worried about that, you know."

Nor scowled. "Maybe I want to die without ever being in love."

Savvy stopped smiling. "Nor," she whispered seriously. "No one wants to die without ever having been in love."

"I've seen you out running around the lake a couple of times," Reed called cordially as he came back. It took Nor a moment to realize he was speaking to her. "You probably haven't seen me. You're a much faster runner than I am." He set a small case on the front counter, pulling out vials of essential oils and handing them to Nor: bergamot, neroli, rosewood.

Nor kept her focus on the vials to avoid both Reed's gaze and Savvy's. "Oh?" she murmured.

"Would you—" He paused and ducked his head to

meet her eyes. "Would you ever consider letting me join you sometime?"

Nor lost the ability to speak as soon as their eyes met. *Please focus, Nor,* she begged herself. What was he asking? To go running? With her? Why did he want to do that? And then, because she couldn't think of anything else to say, she whispered, "Okay."

He examined her for a moment, still holding one of the vials between them. "I'm glad you stuck around, Nor Blackburn," he finally said.

"Where else would I go?" she blurted, incredulous.

He laughed, and it was like a warm beam of sunshine on a cool morning. At that moment, Nor wanted nothing more than to make Reed Oliveira laugh like that again.

And it terrified her.

4

Summoning Spell

"It is important to remember some things
simply do not want to come when they are called.
To force them would be a dire mistake."
—Rona Blackburn

In the spring of 1998, Madge Shimizu, an undergrad student working toward a degree in botany at a notable East Coast university, randomly received an anonymous and innocuous chain letter. The chain letter, like most in those days, promised that even the wildest of Madge's dreams would come true, if only she were to send a copy of the letter out to ten people and one back to the letter's original sender. Though bright, young Madge was also exceedingly superstitious, so she promptly copied the letter eleven times and popped them all into the mail. While she didn't truly believe that a chain letter could affect the outcome of her life, her bright and promising future wasn't something with which she was willing to take any risks.

Besides, what harm could sending out a few letters do?

Much to her surprise, Madge quickly received a note of gratitude from the chain letter's original source, a lonely, pregnant seventeen-year-old girl living on an isolated island off the Washington coast. Through their ensuing correspondence, Madge learned the poor girl had few friends. And as she wasn't very close to her mother, she said, she had very little support at home. The girl felt utterly and completely alone. The chain letter, Madge surmised, had been the girl's attempt to connect with the outside world in search of someone to nurture her, which Madge was happy to do. It seemed particularly auspicious that the girl's name was that of a plant.

A few months after the girl's baby was born, Madge did something that baffled even herself. Instead of taking her semester final exams, Madge packed up her Volvo and moved to the island with every intention of saving the young mother and infant daughter from a life of isolation, neglect, and hopelessness.

It was during her long cross-country drive that Madge realized that the chain letter had worked: her wildest dreams *were* coming true. It was just that her dreams of a college degree and a career in botany were tame ones. If Madge's future was to be bright and promising, she somehow knew that her life had to be built around only one thing: Fern Blackburn.

Upon arriving, Madge discovered that she wasn't the only

61

one from whom Fern had evoked a noble sense of sympathy. In fact, Fern had been corresponding with naive college students like Madge all over the country. And like Madge, they arrived in early spring—the group hovering somewhere between ten and thirty. They brought small camp stoves, heavy dark-green tarpaulins, and portable toilets that failed by mid-July. They filled nights with the sounds of drum circles and lovemaking. They brought dogs with coats ratty with mange that Judd managed to heal and an outbreak of gonorrhea she couldn't. More importantly, they brought their devotion and their idolatry, and most of all a perverse desire to do whatever it took to make Fern happy.

Fern's Followers, as they called themselves, stayed until the heavy October rains brought their tents down around them. After that, only the most devoted remained, which included Madge. She was no doubt already Fern's lover by that point. Nor had never been sure whether Madge was in love with Fern of her own accord or because Fern had wanted her to be and so made it so.

This was Fern's gift: the formidable ability to manipulate the minds of those around her.

At Fern's "suggestion," Madge took the money she'd been saving for a backpacking trip through Europe and rented out an empty storefront on Meandering Lane. A card table was set out front with a sign offering palm readings for five dollars apiece, and the back room was used as a living space. They transformed a small closet into a nursery after

Fern, having seen the obvious affection Judd and Apothia were developing for baby Nor, left the Tower and took the baby with her. It didn't matter that Fern had no genuine interest in motherhood. That was one of the things about Fern: once she knew someone wanted something, she had to have it simply so the other person could not.

Most of Nor's childhood memories were of that small storefront, that closet nursery, and a parade of strange people. She had known some of them by the whimsical names they gave themselves: Summersong, Lake, Vega, Wintersweet. She remembered the clack of the wooden beads that had once hung from the doorway between the front and back rooms, the small hot plate and microwave oven that had made up their kitchen, and the pedestal sink where they'd brushed their teeth and washed their dishes. She remembered the ripped leather sofa against the wall and how the floor was always slippery with down sleeping bags. The little closet where she had slept was draped in brightly colored tapestries; a watermark stained the ceiling. Her bed, a twin-size mattress, had taken up the entire closet floor.

It had been Madge who took care of Nor, Madge who was more mother to her than anyone else in those days, Madge who usually put Nor to bed — making sure she'd brushed her teeth at that sink, that her pajamas were clean. Occasionally it was Vega and his boyfriend Lake, who had a fondness for bedtime stories. Summersong made Nor sleep sachets filled with crushed lavender and rosebuds.

Wintersweet liked to serenade her to sleep, plucking chords on a mandolin and singing Spanish love songs in a soft, wavering soprano. Everyone but Fern had delighted in playing mother to Fern's child. Except when they hadn't. Listening to the raucous laughter outside her little closet, she sometimes waited for someone to remember she was still there. On those days, Nor was left to put herself to bed.

Though Nor had always gone to sleep alone, she sometimes woke up next to Fern. It was strange for Nor to see her mother asleep — docile and quiet, her blond hair lying limp across the pillow, her dreams fluttering behind purple eyelids.

One night, Nor had opened her eyes to find her mother staring at her. Fern verbally dissected Nor's face, pointing out the parts that were hers, the parts that were Nor's father's.

"This," she said, pointing to the dimple in Nor's left cheek or the arch of Nor's eyebrow, "is mine. And this," she said, running her finger down the slope of Nor's nose, "is your father's."

Any ugly parts left over came from Judd.

Afterward, Nor had gazed at herself in the mirror, wondering if she'd recognize the parts of her in her father's face if she ever saw him. That Saturday, she wandered through the farmers' market, trying to recognize her nose in the faces of the men in the crowd.

Another night, Fern had shaken Nor awake and taken her to the fire escape. They'd lain down on the roof, and Fern had pointed out the constellations, both the real ones she could remember and the ones she made up entirely.

"Don't you think I should have everything I want?" Fern whispered. "That even the stars should burn a little brighter, Nor? Just for me. Just because I want them to?"

And with a flick of her wrist, the stars had intensified. The night sky became brighter and brighter until it hurt to look up at all. When the roof caught fire, Nor fled from the blaze, tripping over her blanket as her mother laughed — an eerie, high-pitched laugh that echoed over the sleeping street — and held her palms to the flames until they cracked and blistered.

It was there, watching Fern boil her own skin, that Nor had first learned to fear her mother.

The years went by, and eventually a few more of Fern's devoted followers moved away. First Summersong and then, much to Vega's dismay, Lake left the island as well. Still, Madge's store, now called the Witching Hour, continued to grow. Their apothecary section not only carried common herbs like lavender, sage, and thyme, but soon more obscure plants that Madge grew herself. Wormwood and mugwort were good for hexes; anise seed and feverfew for protection spells; mandrake root to bless the home; and calendula to bless the heart. None of their spells ever worked, but people bought them anyway.

The Witching Hour's popularity soared with the start of their guided walking tours, the first a lantern-lit trip to the cemetery on Halloween. They held festivals celebrating the pagan holidays, and every Sunday morning, the back room that was their home served as a passable space for private palm readings.

Fern's involvement in the store was sporadic at best. When she was bored, which was often, she got a kick out of tricking customers into purchasing expensive teas she claimed had healing properties. She'd take their hands and stroke their health lines with her ragged nails.

"It's specially blended," she'd purr. "Tailored to what I discern an individual needs." Then she'd go into the back, pour some of Madge's discarded chamomile tea into a Styrofoam cup, and present it with a flourish to the unsuspecting customer. Sometimes it wouldn't even be tea at all, but coffee or chicken broth or, once, some Diet Coke. The customer would take a tentative sip and then regard Fern with disbelieving eyes, declaring themselves cured of whatever ailed them: tendinitis, athlete's foot, heartbreak, loneliness. Of course, they'd believed it because Fern wanted them to. And Fern could get anything she wanted.

Anything but Nor's father. For reasons Fern couldn't comprehend, Quinn Sweeney was impervious to her powers.

A descendant of the island's original port master, Quinn Sweeney was handsome and well-liked for his gentle temperament. He had an aptitude for classical piano, for which he'd received a full scholarship from a reputable music school far away from Anathema Island. While in high school, Quinn had spent Saturdays working alongside his mother at the Sweet and Savory Bakery and Sundays playing the pipe organ for several churches throughout the archipelago. Twice a month, he volunteered to teach music lessons to disadvantaged children.

Nor always wondered what he must have thought when Fern Blackburn suddenly began starring in his dreams at night. Fern Blackburn, the girl who slept in the back of the class. Fern Blackburn, the girl with low-slung jeans and exposed hip bones, whose loose-fitting tank tops barely covered the sides of her breasts. It was only a matter of time before he'd found himself approaching her front door. Had he any idea why he winced at each crunch of gravel beneath his furtive footsteps, or why the back of his neck was slick with sweat? And when she'd greeted him by placing her mouth on his, was he wondering what he was doing there at all?

Before Fern, Quinn Sweeney had always dated nice girls. Girls with shiny ponytails and straight teeth. Girls who came from respectable families and dreamed of pink prom dresses and white stretch limousines. Girls who'd left him panting with gentlemanly desire because he was afraid to touch them, afraid to ask, and afraid to question for fear he'd offend them. Those nice girls had never climbed on top of him and huskily asked, "What do you want?" or whispered, "Tell me how to please you," their breath hot in his ear.

For three days, Quinn and Fern remained locked in

her bedroom in the Tower, consumed entirely with each other's mouths, hands, fingers, and tongues. During the few moments when Fern had allowed him to sleep, she'd traced his handsome features with her fingers, as if laying claim to him.

But at the end of those three days, Quinn Sweeney left. Just like all the others before him. And the next time they saw each other, the only sign Quinn gave that there had been anything between them was a deep flush that spread across his cheeks.

Quinn Sweeney left the island right after he gave his commencement speech and five months before Fern would give birth to Nor. After college, he'd gone on to a marginally successful career in music composition. He had a lovely wife — more kind than she was beautiful — and he never forgot to send his mother a birthday gift. And like all the other fathers before him, Quinn Sweeney never acknowledged the fact that he had fathered a child with a Blackburn daughter.

Rona Blackburn's curse was an impenetrable shield, and try as she might, Fern could not break through it. For years, Quinn Sweeney remained immune to Fern's charismatic powers. But history had a funny and terrible way of repeating itself. The terrible truth was that Fern had fallen in love with Quinn. Desperately wanting him to love her back, a Blackburn woman once again found herself reaching for black magic.

When Nor was nine years old, Fern dragged her once again to the roof of Madge's shop. With the brightened stars burning yellow on her skin, Fern stared across the ocean surrounding their little island and called his name. She called for him over and over again until her sallow skin had glowed purple in the cold.

Nor sat huddled with her hands over her ears and watched her mother carve his name into her skin, just like Rona once had, hoping the wicked sacrifice of her own blood would add potency to her spell.

Nor watched her mother's blood inch its way across the roof, then stop. Weakened and defeated, Fern slumped to the ground as Nor breathed a shaky sigh of relief. Perhaps the madness was finally over. And then Fern looked at her — stared at her — with a terrible smile spreading across her wan face. "Why must it be my blood that's spilled," she mused aloud, "when it could just as easily be yours?"

Nor screamed in pain when the skin on the back of her hands began peeling away. Blood seeped out from under her fingernails and oozed from the corners of her eyes. Nor wiped frantically at her face, smearing blood across her cheeks. Her skin began to tear open at her wrists and elbows, like a rag doll splitting at the seams.

I'm dying, Nor thought. A sticky film coated the back of her throat, and breathing became difficult. Unconsciousness fell over her like a shroud. She could faintly make out the sound of Madge stumbling onto the roof, pleading for Fern to let Nor go. And then, when Nor was certain her mother never would, when death, in fact, seemed inevitable, Fern herself collapsed.

Nor gulped fresh air into her lungs. Madge ripped off her sweater and pressed it against Nor's wounds. A red stain spread across the wool. The roof beneath Nor was slick and wet with blood, but whether it was her mother's blood or her own, she couldn't tell. At that moment, it seemed there was nothing in Nor's world but blood and pain.

Vega carried the unconscious Fern downstairs to the couch in the back room, where she slept for three days straight. As the rest of them sat vigil, Nor made her own recovery, tucked safely away in her little closet. Her skin slowly stitched itself back together, leaving only pale pink scars along her wrists and elbows. Nor was also left with a memory of when her mother was willing to sacrifice her. For the first time, she wondered how much pain Fern would be willing to inflict to get what she wanted. She wondered if Fern, in fact, enjoyed the pain of others.

And then, in the early morning of the third day —

A crash in the other room startled Nor awake. She yelped when her own door flew open. Her mother, wild-eyed and terrifying, tore into the closet room and began tossing clothes into a ratty old suitcase.

Nor watched in stunned silence. "What are you doing?"

she dared to ask. She hesitantly reached into the suitcase and made an awkward attempt to organize the mess within.

Fern slapped Nor's hands out of the way. "It finally worked," she hissed. "I've made him come back for me." Fern slammed the suitcase closed.

Nor followed her mother into the shop, her palms sweating and her heart pounding fast in her chest. Everyone else was asleep, and the metallic glow from the headlights of a car parked outside cast their faces in a sickly yellow hue. Nor gazed at Madge's sleeping face, and that was when it hit her. Tears choked her words. "Do we have to leave right now? Can I say good-bye first? To Madge? To Savvy?"

But when she turned around, all she saw was her mother escaping through the front door. In a voice suddenly falsely sweet, Fern called out a greeting to the person in the car waiting for her.

Nor tripped over her feet in her haste to follow. She could see that it was a man in the car, his posture stiff and unnatural. From that distance, what Nor couldn't see were the parts of her that had come from him — the slope of her nose, the shape of her mouth. He had blond hair, like her mother. Nor's hair was dark and thick, like Judd's.

Without another word, Fern took Nor's father away from her, racing toward the ferry dock as if the island might lock itself down before Fern could make her exit.

Nor wasn't sure what to do next. So she waited. She

waited for the dust of the retreating car to settle. She waited for the ferry to pull away and for its bright lights to fade into the dark.

She waited, and with her little heart breaking, she thought of all the time she spent waiting—waiting for someone to notice her, waiting for someone to care whether she was sick or hungry. Or scared.

Finally, from the opposite direction, she saw a tiny pinprick of light approach. It grew larger and larger until she recognized it as the glow from the end of a pipe.

A formidable woman peered down at Nor. "Well, let's go then, girlie," she said.

Nor sniffed and wiped her nose with the back of her hand. "Where are we going?"

"Home."

"Home?"

"Yes. Apothia's got your room all ready for you."

"I have a room?" Nor asked, surprised.

Judd harrumphed. "Of course you have a room. It's been waiting for you for almost ten years. I think that's about long enough, don't you?"

Nor nodded and placed her tiny hand in her grandmother's large calloused one. And that was when Nor realized that someone else had been waiting as well.

But this time, that someone else had been waiting for *her*.

5

Benevolence Spell

"Any decent human being, witch or otherwise,
has the capacity to do good in this world. It's merely
a case of whether one chooses to do so."
— Rona Blackburn

Nor woke to a cold gray October sky peering down at her through the skylight. After sticking her arm out from her cocoon of blankets, she blindly groped for her phone and peeked at its clock. She groaned. She was supposed to open the shop today, and she was already late.

Bijou enjoyed the warmth of the blankets while she got up and threw on an oversize black sweater and a pair of jeans. The jeans had seen better days, and she promptly caught her foot on a frayed tear in one of the knees, ripping an even larger hole in the worn fabric.

A few minutes later, a piece of slightly burned marmalade toast in each hand, Nor hurried down Meandering Lane toward the Witching Hour.

She found a group of impatient customers waiting for her on the front steps — Savvy was first in line. Her lime-green Afro puffed out around her head like a dandelion clock. She was eating a gooey, frosted cinnamon bun. "You're late," she scolded cheerfully as she chewed.

"What are all these people doing here?" Nor muttered. There was always an increased number of sightseers in October — it was the last chance for whale watching — but today it seemed unusually busy, especially for a Tuesday morning. With growing anxiety, Nor worried it had nothing to do with the migrating whales.

"So you don't know," Savvy said.

"Don't know what?" Nor opened the door to the shop, nearly toppling a display of her mother's book. The candles and colorful flowers arranged around it brought to mind a shrine, as did the way the customers all flocked to it.

"Nor, you *have* to get a new phone." Savvy sighed. "You're living in the dark ages."

"I like my phone."

"Your phone is complete shit."

"That's why I like it," Nor grumbled. "What's the big deal anyway?"

"The big deal is that some famous YouTuber endorsed your mother's book. Hence"— Savvy gestured to the crowded store —"all of this."

"And what did this YouTuber say?"

"Basically, she bought a spell from your mother's book, just for the hell of it. But it turns out the spell worked — she had this horrible scar on her leg from some accident she was in as a child, and it completely disappeared! In seconds! Like poof! Gone. Can you believe it?"

A lump formed in Nor's throat. The scars on her wrists and elbows began to hum, and she tried not to think about the pair of scissors in the drawer underneath the counter. Could she believe it? Of course she could. Nor was quite certain her mother could cause snakes to fall from the sky if she wanted.

Savvy picked up a copy of Fern's book and flipped through the pages. "Is it true?" she asked. "Could your mom really do *this?*"

Nor glanced at the page Savvy was tapping with her bright-yellow fingernail. Her heart sank; that page featured the Resurrection Spell.

"Please don't tell me you think this is anything but bullshit," Nor said.

Savvy's eyes suddenly narrowed. "So what if I do?"

Nor shrugged. "You're too smart for that. Besides, even if my mom could do all of this — and I'm not saying she can — do you really think it would come without a cost?"

"I *know* it doesn't," Savvy said sarcastically. "There's an actual price listed for each spell."

"That's not what I meant. The fact that you lost your

mom doesn't make you unique, Savvy. It makes you an easy target." Nor regretted saying it as soon as the words had left her mouth.

"That was a cheap shot," Savvy said quietly.

"You're right," Nor agreed quickly. She gently took the book from Savvy and set it to the side. "This book isn't going to help anyone, Savvy. If anything, I think it'll only exploit people's pain. I don't want that to happen to you."

I don't want my mom to hurt you, too.

Savvy nodded and stared wistfully at the book on the counter. "Do you think your mom would have given me a discount? What with me being your best friend and all?"

"For that she'd probably charge you double." Nor pushed a few dollar bills at Savvy. "I think we need caffeine," she said. "My treat?"

"Okay," Savvy said. "But you're buying me breakfast, too."

"What about that cinnamon bun you just ate?" Nor asked.

"That was just a snack." Savvy gave Nor a small smile before leaving the shop. Somehow it made Nor feel even worse.

Why did I say that about her mom? Nor thought. She balled her hand into a fist until her nails bit into her palm. Nor remembered watching her grandmother try to help Savvy's mom. Judd's hands had been covered in tiny quills and with wisps of Lisbet Dawson's blond hair, but whatever had made her ill had been far stronger than Judd's magic.

Once the store had quieted down a little, Nor opened her mother's book to the Resurrection Spell. From what Nor had heard, it brought people back from the dead, but what they came back as could hardly be called human. They were more like nightmares walking around in some loved one's skin. Nor shuddered to imagine what Savvy's mom might look like if she were brought back: the color leeched from her hair and skin, her eyes dead and cold, her tongue black.

Nor quickly shut the book. If Fern really could cast the Resurrection Spell, she doubted that whoever requested it knew what they were getting.

Over the next few weeks, the success of *The Price Guide to the Occult* expanded at terrifying speed. The YouTuber's endorsement was followed by rave reviews and talk show appearances. Everywhere Nor looked, it seemed, there was her mother, the beautiful woman who could make wishes come true. All the reviewers, the guest bloggers, and everyone who sent in the required fee for a desired spell confirmed that Fern Blackburn was the real deal. *The Price Guide to the Occult* working miracles was the only thing anyone wanted to talk about.

On the evening of Halloween, Nor marched down Meandering Lane after her shift at the Witching Hour. The street was filled with trick-or-treaters. Parents with strollers raced after tiny goblins and ghouls, pirates and princesses. The kids filled their tote bags with pumpkin cookies from the Sweet and Savory Bakery, popcorn balls from the Willowbark General Store, and chocolate bars from the co-op. Strangely, a large bowl of sour candies had been left outside Theo's mechanic shop. Savvy, the self-proclaimed Queen of Halloween who had spent three weeks constructing a papier-mâché head for her sea horse costume last year, was nowhere to be seen.

The cold October air felt crisp in Nor's lungs. The sun had already set. If Judd were out, the porch light would be on. The light was off, which meant, for the first time in days, Judd was at home. Lately, the number of late-night phone calls that drew Judd out for hours at a time had increased; it sometimes seemed as though Nor and Apothia lived alone in that great tower. It was difficult not to feel Judd's absence; she was a woman who took up a great deal of space.

Judd was taking Fern's ascent to fame as well as expected, which meant she was not taking it well at all. She had gotten particularly irate after reading a glowing blog post about *The Price Guide to the Occult*, and now the keys on Apothia's laptop looked like broken teeth. After that, Apothia had put a ban on any mention of Fern or the book.

Though an argument between Judd and Fern wasn't anything Nor wanted to witness personally, she was certain that should it come to that, her mother would be no match for the Giantess. At least that was what she kept telling herself.

Besides noticing the porch light, Nor saw a familiar

turquoise Vespa in the driveway, a matching helmet resting on the seat. She could hear Bijou and Antiquity barking inside the house, but it wasn't the dogs that greeted her at the door. It was Savvy. Her lilac hair extensions hung sleekly down one shoulder; the color made for a pretty contrast to her reddish-brown skin.

"What are you doing here?" Nor asked. "You know I don't celebrate Halloween."

"Which is why we're not celebrating Halloween." Savvy smiled that conspiratorial smile of hers and moved to the side.

The dining room had been completely transformed. A rich tapestry covered the table. Each place had been set with Apothia's fine china, delicately painted with dragons and songbirds and tiny teahouses. There were goblets edged in rose gold, white pumpkins, and tiny bouquets of marigolds and chrysanthemums and gerbera daisies. Fairy lights swung gently from the ceiling, and the light from dozens of candles danced across the walls.

"You have Savannah to thank for all this," Apothia said, nodding toward Savvy. "It was her idea."

"Think of it as a way of making up for all those birthdays you haven't let us celebrate," Savvy scolded. "All those missed birthday cakes. Such a damn shame."

Having never gotten accustomed to celebrating her birthdays — Fern wasn't really the type of mother for balloons and birthday cake — Nor had been planning on spending the evening of her seventeenth birthday doing what she did every year. Absolutely nothing.

"Turning seventeen isn't that big a deal," Nor said.

"Well, we won't be able to throw you a party next year," Savvy said. "You'll be eighteen, so you'll be too busy voting. And buying cigarettes. And going to jail after committing a felony."

"That should be one hell of a birthday," Apothia said.

Nor smiled and looked around. "Will Judd be here tonight?" she asked.

Apothia nodded. "Of course. She helped me with the cake."

Sitting in the middle of the table was a cake unlike any other cake Nor had ever seen. A layer of raspberry jam was spread between each of its three tiers, and it had been not just topped with frosting, but drizzled with honey and candied figs. Whoever made it certainly had a much more delicate touch and discerning eye than Judd. "No, she didn't," Nor said.

"Well, no, she didn't," Apothia admitted. "But that's really for the best, don't you think?"

Nor nodded, distracted suddenly by the suspiciously high number of place settings around the table. "Who else did you invite?"

"People," Savvy answered quickly. She splayed her tiny hands across Nor's back and pushed her up the stairs. "Now, enough with the questions. You'll ruin my surprise!"

As soon as Nor's bedroom door closed behind them, Savvy dropped to the floor and rummaged through the hot-pink backpack she had carried up with her.

Nor waited for a moment before asking, "This surprise isn't like, *Surprise, you have to wear a costume,* is it? You know I don't do costumes."

"It hurts me every time you say that," Savvy said. "But no, we will not be donning costumes this year."

"Then what will we be doing?"

"It's your birthday," Savvy said, pulling a yellow corset out of the backpack. "It's your birthday, and while I know costumes are *verboten,* you are still not wearing"—she pointed to Nor—"that."

Nor looked down: ripped jeans and mud-splattered combat boots. Her hair was certainly its usual mess. Then she looked at Savvy: lilac unicorn mane, stud-encrusted sweater dress, thigh-high lace-up boots. If Nor had to pinpoint who between them had magic in her blood, she'd pick Savvy over herself in a heartbeat. "Good point."

"It's like you're allergic to color," Savvy muttered, flipping quickly through Nor's closet. She paused briefly at a strapless bustier dress she'd bought Nor the previous year, certain that by doing so she could somehow coax her into wearing it, and gave Nor a hopeful glance.

"Not a chance in hell."

Savvy sighed and returned to her backpack. Nor watched in amazement as Savvy pulled out one oddity after another:

81

ripped lace leggings. Fingerless gloves. A mesh halter top.

Nor picked up a pair of discarded leather hot pants. "Are you sure I can't just wear something I already own? Something I actually *wear*?"

From her backpack, Savvy took out a transparent platform shoe with a plastic goldfish floating in the heel. "If Goth ever becomes fashionable again, you'll be the first person I call. For now, though —" Savvy looked into the bag again. "Ha!" she said triumphantly, and yanked something out.

It was a blue velvet slip dress with tiny spaghetti straps, the blue so dark it almost looked black. Almost. It was also beautiful and feminine and unlike anything Nor had ever worn before, which, judging from the expression on Savvy's face, was entirely the point.

"It's pretty," Nor admitted. "But —"

Savvy quickly dug through Nor's closet and took out a long black cardigan. "With this thrown over it? What do you think?"

"Does it *really* matter what I'm wearing?"

"Trust me. It matters," Savvy said. "I might have invited my very good friend Grayson. And he might be bringing his brother along. Who might be, you know, your almost lover, Reed Oliveira."

"What?" Nor balked. "You're sure they're coming? *Both* of them?"

"Surprise," Savvy said, and held up the dress.

Nor scowled, but snatched it out of her friend's hand.

When she slipped it over her head, she found the hem stopped a few inches above her knee. It was short, but for something they had pulled out of her petite friend's wardrobe, it wasn't nearly as short as Nor had been expecting. She quickly slid on the sweater, thankful that its sleeves were long enough to cover her wrists. With expert hands, Savvy twisted Nor's wild waist-long hair into loose curls that extended down her back, and then lined her eyes in shimmery black.

"This is going to be so great," Savvy said resolutely.

Nor sighed quietly. How could anything be great when Nor could practically feel her mother's breath on the back of her neck? Anything that even slightly resembled happiness seemed dangerous, as if cloaking herself in misery was the only way she could protect herself from the dark gloom of her mother's lurking shadow. For Nor, feeling happy felt like being a glaring target. Feeling happy meant that she had something to lose.

"Look, Nor, I love you, but you're not exactly the easiest person to get to know." Savvy stared at Nor and drummed her purple-lacquered nails against her lips. "I swear, sometimes it's like you have the ability to turn yourself invisible."

Nor grimaced. She slipped on her combat boots, hiding the scars on her ankles. Yes, that was exactly what she did. Not on purpose. It just happened sometimes.

"But Reed Oliveira did notice you. And for once, we,"

Savvy said, grabbing Nor's arm and dragging her down the stairs, "and by we, I mean *you*, are going to take full advantage of that situation."

"*You* notice me," Nor grumbled.

Savvy turned back and smiled, the silver hoop in her eyebrow glinting merrily in the glow of the candles and fairy lights at the bottom of the stairs. "Yeah, but I'm nosy. I notice everything."

6

Love Spell

"Unlike bread, there is no easy recipe for love.
The unfortunate truth is either one has it or one does not."
— Rona Blackburn

Nor followed Savvy into the dining room and saw that a few of her guests had already arrived — including Reed. There was a part of her that was afraid that if she took even one step into the room, he'd disappear. Which would have been such a shame. *He makes the rest of the world look like a watercolor painting,* Nor thought. *All blurred lines and swirling colors.* She grimaced.

"Oh, get a grip, Nor," she muttered, and forced herself down the stairs.

Fortunately for her, Reed didn't disappear. Instead, he came over to her and fished a small box out of one of his pockets. "I didn't know what to get you," he explained, handing it to her.

"You didn't have to get me anything," Nor said.

"Yeah, he did," Grayson called from across the room. He helped himself to a candied fig, then added, "What kind of loser shows up to a birthday party without a gift?"

"What did *you* bring?" Savvy shot back at Grayson.

"Nothing," he admitted candidly, coming to stand with them. "But I'm not trying to impress anyone."

Reed's cheeks turned pink, and he smacked his brother on the side of the head. "Shut up, Grayson."

Rubbing his head, Grayson looked over at Savvy and said, "He changed his shirt, like, four times." Reed clocked him again. "Stop!"

Savvy rolled her eyes and pointed at the box in Nor's hand. "Open it," she ordered.

After pulling off the top of the box, Nor peered inside at what looked like — a bronzed crow's foot? "Oh." She was unsure what to say. She picked it up and examined it more closely. The talons were curled inward, clutching a translucent stone. "Thank you?"

"What *is* that thing?" Grayson exclaimed. He shook his head at Reed. "*This* is what you got her? A dead bird's foot? Man, how is it that you've ever had a girlfriend?"

This time it was Savvy who punched him. She took the claw out of the box and slid it along her little finger. "*I* think it looks like a ring," she said, waving her hand at Nor.

"I don't think it's a ring," Reed was quick to say. "I don't know what it is. I found it over at the Society and thought it was weird and that you'd appreciate it."

"Because *I'm weird?*" Nor asked, horrified.

"Only in the best way possible," he reassured her.

Nor felt her own cheeks flush, and she slid the unusual present into her pocket for safekeeping — or at least until she could figure out what the hell to do with it.

She glanced across the room at Judd and Apothia, bickering over lighting the candles on the cake. In the corner, Antiquity growled softly in her sleep. A knock on the door announced Madge's arrival. As Savvy launched into some animated story, Nor's fingers found Reed's present in her pocket. And in spite of the sense of foreboding she couldn't seem to shake, Nor smiled, a real smile.

Hours later, the full moon shone its silvery light through the dining room window. Most of the candles had burned out, and the tablecloth was dotted with hardened puddles of melted wax. All that remained of the cake were plates smeared with frosting and raspberry jam. Several empty bottles of Apothia's plum wine littered the table. Madge had left a while ago.

"You know our midnight tour on Samhain is our most popular tour of the year," Madge had apologized, kissing Nor on the cheek.

At the head of the table, Judd leaned back in her chair,

smoking her pipe and filling the air with the sweet aroma of her tobacco. Apothia disappeared into the parlor, and then the sweeping music of Tchaikovsky's *Swan Lake* filled the room. Nor and her grandmother shared a good-humored groan as Apothia jetéd and fouettéd back into the room. She tried to coax Judd to dance, but instead, Judd pulled Apothia onto her lap. Apothia took Judd's face in her hands, and they kissed to catcalls from Savvy and Grayson.

Nor would normally have been embarrassed by their public display, but glancing around the room, all she saw was joy. It was in the flush of Apothia's soft cheeks and in Savvy's chirpy voice and the lively movement of her hands. It was in her grandmother's eyes, in the contented sighs of both dogs asleep under the table, and in the clumsy manner in which Grayson attempted to sneak another glass of wine. It was in the way Reed laughed, silently, his shoulders shaking and his eyes squinted shut.

Eventually Judd and Apothia headed upstairs to bed. As Savvy blew out the last of the candles, Nor and Reed stacked the dirty plates and collected the silverware. Grayson feigned sleep at the end of the table until they were finished.

"I was just resting my eyes," he insisted.

"You were just trying to get out of doing any of the work," Savvy said.

"Well, yeah. That, too."

Outside, the air was rich with chimney smoke; Nor could practically taste the cinders. It was a familiar scent that Nor associated with the season, when the creeping cold brought fireplaces back to life.

Nor pulled her sweater more tightly around herself. From the Tower's front porch, she could see the rush of the waves against the beach below. There was movement out there as well, and she could hear a chorus of low, ethereal moans echoing across the water.

"Apparently all the humpback whales in the area sing the same song," Reed said, coming up behind her. He brushed up against her arm, and Nor's pulse began to flutter. "Kind of like they have their own dialect or something."

"There's no way those are *all* whales," said Grayson, who'd also stepped outside. He pointed to more shadowy shapes in the water, including several close to shore.

"It pains me to admit this," Savvy said, "but I think he might be right."

"What are they then?" Reed asked.

Nor left the others on the porch and went into the yard, away from the light of the Tower and to listen more clearly to the mournful song of the whales and whatever other creatures were out there. She definitely heard a hint of something different in the whales' voices. *Something restive*, Nor thought. The hair on the back of her neck started to prickle. *Something dark and disquieting.*

Without a word to the other three, Nor walked to the edge of the property and pushed her way through the overgrowth until she found the trail leading down to the beach.

A mess of brambles and naked tree limbs crisscrossed over her head, forming a tunnel that made Nor feel like she was in a scene from *Alice in Wonderland*.

The trail was unusually overgrown, as if the forest had turned suddenly savage. The plants greeted Nor with hostility and snagged her exposed skin with sharp thorns and stinging nettles. Nor didn't remember the trail ever being this difficult to navigate.

Behind her, someone cursed. The thistles must have gotten them as well.

Nor stopped at the end of the trail and waited for everyone else to emerge. A piece of Grayson's sweatshirt had been torn. Reed had scratches on his cheeks, and Savvy had one across her forehead.

The beach stretched two miles in either direction, connecting with Meandering Lane at one end and with a small inlet leading to Celestial Lake at the other. Though not the most beautiful, the beach had its own kind of triumphs — the view of the archipelago being one of them. The water glittered in the moonlight like diamonds. Squinting, Nor could spy the barnacle-covered tail of a humpback whale. The faint whine of a powerboat could be heard in the distance.

Grayson took off toward the water's edge, Savvy following closely behind him. She shrieked every time one of her bootheels got trapped in between the rocks.

"Shall we?" Reed asked. He held out his hand, and Nor suddenly wished she could push a giant pause button and suspend time. In that moment, she didn't want to think about her mother or about whatever was going on out there in that cold water; all she wanted to think about was that Reed Oliveira was holding his hand out to her. And for a moment, time did exactly that. It paused. And then Nor stepped off the path, slipped her hand into Reed's, and followed him onto the beach.

"I was right," Grayson called. "Those aren't just whales."

"What are they then? Mermaids?" Savvy teased.

"No, not mermaids," Grayson snapped.

The tinny whine of the powerboat grew louder as it cut through the waves. It shined a spotlight over a cluster of creatures in the water. Nor could make out breaching Dall's porpoises, and the long extended arms of a giant Pacific octopus waving wildly like the mythological kraken. Jet-black dorsal fins revealed the largest orca pod Nor had ever seen. Barking steller sea lions, harbor seals, and otters dove in and out of the waves. Sea birds glided overhead, their eerie witch cackles filling the sky.

They were all moving in the same direction. They were all moving north toward the Pacific Ocean, as if they were all running from a common enemy invading the cold waters of the archipelago.

"I've never seen anything like this," Reed said.

"Maybe they know something we don't." Savvy teetered warily away from the shore. "Like the way dogs act really weird before an earthquake is about to hit?"

While the others debated their own theories, Nor shut her eyes and tuned them out. The thoughts of all those sea creatures trickled over her like water in a creek. At first, it was hard to separate one creature's thoughts from another. She quickly realized it didn't matter, that they were all conveying basically the same thing.

Nor paled, and her skin prickled with horripilation. Still clutching Reed's hand, she backed away from the water's edge, fear piercing her like a thousand arrows.

Savvy's right, she realized with a start. *They're afraid of something that's drawing nearer.* They were afraid in the way a herd is afraid when a predator stalks them, readying to pick them off one by one. Something out there, something dangerous and unnatural, had them spooked.

The powerboat had finally bumped its way to shore. Nor recognized the girl at the helm as Charlie Coldwater, her cousin Gage beside her. She cut the engine sharply just as a Jeep, almost as dilapidated as the old boat, rumbled down the beach toward them, sending an arc of rocks over their heads, and stopped.

"Hey!" Savvy called indignantly. "What the hell?"

The Jeep was yellow but thickly splattered with mud. Both doors and the roof were missing. The driver, a tall young man with chiseled features, slammed the Jeep into park and leaped out almost before the vehicle came to a complete stop. The passenger, on the other hand, seemed uninterested in what was happening in the water, though it was hard to tell behind his dark aviator sunglasses.

"Well?" the driver of the Jeep called to the Coldwaters.

"They're moving out fast," Charlie called back. "They keep going at this rate, there won't be anything left out here but anemones and barnacles."

Gage swung out over the side of the boat and hauled it onto the beach by a soggy rope.

The driver of the Jeep considered Charlie's words for a moment. "Any sharks?"

"Oh yeah, loads," Gage said, "but they're not preying on any of the others. They all just seem pretty fixated on getting the hell out of here."

The Jeep driver turned to his passenger. "What do you think?"

The passenger shrugged, his back still to the shore, and spit some sunflower shells onto the rocks. "We could just ask the girl," he finally said.

At that, Gage sneered. "What's she going to tell us? I doubt she has a clue about what's going on."

The driver leaned against the Jeep, crossed his arms, and turned to Nor. "Well?" he asked her.

In an instant, all eyes were on Nor, but she was just as caught off guard as they were. *She* was "the girl"? "I — I don't know!" Nor stuttered, but she did, sort of. Still, how did these strangers know to ask her why the animals were so spooked?

"No shit," Gage said. "See, Pike? What did I tell you?"

"Why are you picking on her?" Savvy said, coming to Nor's defense. "Go find a marine biologist and be an asshole to them, why don't you?"

Gage gave Nor a knowing smirk before turning back to Pike. "Like I said."

Why is this guy such an asshole? Nor thought. She glared at him, but no matter how long or how intensely she scowled, he refused to look at her. As badly as she wanted to shut him up for good, when she saw the look on Savvy's face, she quickly decided against saying anything more. The fact that there were sea creatures all but running over one another in their haste to get away from the archipelago was alarming enough.

Pike shook his head. "Man, shut up, Gage." He called to Charlie, still sitting in the boat: "We'll meet you two back at the compound."

Glowering, Gage splashed back into the water and launched himself over the side of the boat. The word *Arcana* had been carefully painted on the back of the wooden boat in gold swirling letters. The motor started with a rumble. Charlie squared her baseball hat, and the two Coldwaters took off, the small boat bouncing along the waves and disappearing into the dark.

"Just ignore him," Pike said to Nor. "It's common

knowledge that our cousin is — well." He turned to the passenger still spitting sunflower seeds into the sand. "What would you say he is, Sena Crowe?"

"He's a dick."

Pike laughed. "Exactly." He swung back into the driver's seat, and after a few false starts, the Jeep sputtered to life. "You should get back," he called to Nor and her friends over the churning engine. "It is Halloween. Who knows what else is lurking out here in the dark." And with that, the Jeep disappeared in another spray of sand and rocks.

Savvy spun toward Nor. "What the hell is that guy's problem?"

Good question, Nor thought. They seemed to know more about her than she knew about them. Nor forced herself to shrug, hoping a mask of cool indifference would hide the tremor in her hands. She jammed them into the pockets of her sweater just in case. "No idea," she said.

"Well, I'm pretty sure I hate him." Savvy looked out at the water and shuddered. "Can we go? This is starting to give me the creeps."

"I thought we liked things that give us the creeps," Nor teased.

"Not this."

"Maybe we should take the long way back," Reed suggested, fingering the cuts on his face. "I'm not sure I'm up for more blood loss."

Nor smiled, but she didn't trust herself to say anything.

The worrying change in the island's wildlife — and how much the Coldwaters seemed to know about her — fluttered like a butterfly in the pit of her stomach. With everything that had happened tonight, she was afraid that if she opened her mouth that butterfly, all of her secrets, all the parts of herself she wanted to keep hidden — most especially from Reed — would come pouring out.

Reed took Nor's hand, and she let him guide her down the beach while she tuned in to the faint cries in the water, of sea lions and a gray whale. Savvy was right. They did know something. There was something coming, something to fear. Nor wondered if the island's residents should have been running away from Anathema Island, too.

Reed and Nor's pace was far slower than that of Savvy and Grayson; soon, the two of them were alone, weaving their way silently along the shoreline. They reached a wide dirt road that led them up to Meandering Lane. On either side of them, beach grass glowed silver and ethereal in the moonlight. The grass moaned like a ghost in the wind — a hollow, grief-stricken sound. It chilled Nor to the bone.

The sound of voices carried over from the other side of the island. The lantern lights from the Witching Hour's midnight tour of the cemetery moved across the black landscape like a constellation. What would happen if they actually succeeded in summoning the ghost of a Blackburn daughter? If Astrid, Judd's mother, or Hester, the first daughter, appeared? Would they be able to tell Nor what was going on? Would they be able to protect them from whatever dark force the animals were so afraid of?

Outside the Tower, they paused, and Reed ran his hands up and down Nor's arms as if to warm them. She tugged at the sleeves of her sweater, making sure they covered her scars, then reached up and pressed her hand lightly against the scratches on Reed's face and felt the stubble on his cheeks.

"They don't look too bad," Nor started to say — and then gasped softly when the scratches on his face disappeared at her touch. She pulled her hand away in alarm as pain, delicate as freshly mown blades of grass, fluttered to the ground. *Shit.* She hadn't meant to do that. She needed to be more careful.

Fortunately, Reed didn't seem to notice either her reaction or that she'd healed his cheek. And instead of running away, spooked by this girl who was more than simply *weird*, he kissed her cheek good night, pressing his lips just close enough to Nor's ear to send shivers down her neck.

7

Calamity Spell

"Disaster can come in all shapes and sizes.
It's best to be prepared."
— Rona Blackburn

A few days after Nor's seventeenth birthday, her mother was scheduled to appear on a popular morning talk show. Despite Nor's initial intention — that there was no way in *hell* she was going to acknowledge the highly publicized event, let alone watch it — in the end, the temptation was an itch she had to scratch. With an exasperated sigh, she sat up in bed, pushed her wild hair out of her eyes, and turned on her phone.

She launched the search engine, typed in her mother's name, and after scrolling through the hundreds of hits that came up, found what she was looking for. And then there she was, her comely face filling the cracked screen of Nor's cell phone: Fern Blackburn. The host oohed and aahed along with the delighted studio audience as, in the blink of an eye, Fern transformed a homely young woman into a beauty almost as fetching as Fern herself. Then a child, stripped of her sight as an infant, saw her parents for the first time. The only thing missing from the show was a lame man dropping his crutches and walking across the stage.

"How stunning you are," the host crooned. "And yet how humble." Everyone in the audience murmured their approval of this striking visionary who would selflessly guide them all into the light of the future. That Fern Blackburn could make wishes come true was no longer in doubt.

Nor squinted at the screen, searching her mother's face for any signs of the incredible strain and sacrifice Nor knew was necessary for Fern to perform such "miracles." She saw none and grew more alarmed. There was nothing, not a single flaw, not a bruise or a blemish, not even a broken capillary. Only fern tattoos spiraling across her porcelain skin. Nor remembered what her mother had had to do in the past to practice magic outside her own Burden. She remembered being on the roof with Fern that night. She remembered how her mother's skin had split open, how her mother's blood had trickled across the roof. And she remembered how the blood had poured from the wounds Fern had then made on Nor's skin when her own blood wasn't enough. If Fern wasn't paying the price for her spells herself, then someone else certainly was.

The audience rose to its feet and applauded. Nor turned off her phone in disgust and tried not to think about the terrible cost someone had paid for restoring that little girl's sight.

Nor shuffled downstairs and found Apothia in the kitchen preparing a tray of assorted breakfast foods: fresh bagels and sliced strawberries, hazelnut spread, and a jar of honey. A greasy-smelling hash sizzled on the stove. There was also orange juice, a pot of what smelled like peppermint tea, a French coffee press, and a pitcher of Bloody Mary mix.

"After seeing Fern's little demonstration on national television," Apothia said, "your grandmother and I decided we needed something to give us strength. We haven't yet decided if that strength will come from food or from vodka."

Through the glass of the parlor door, Nor could make out Judd's massive silhouette, stretched across the small divan.

When she had first moved into the Tower, Nor had seen the parlor only through the wavy lead windows on the door. For generations, the room had been used only at night, during the dark, lonely hours when desperate islanders would arrive with their whispered desires and frantic pleas. Those few times when the door had been left open, all those trapped, desperate voices had rushed out in gusts of *I must haves* and *please help mes* and *I can't live withouts* like a wretched case of bad breath.

Apothia placed her hand, soft and dry, against Nor's forehead as if checking for fever. "You look pale," she fretted, her eyes flicking over the scarred skin peeking out from along the collar of Nor's pajamas.

"You always say that," Nor muttered, popping a sliced bagel onto a plate. Slathering it with hazelnut spread and sliced strawberries, she considered telling Apothia about the strangely vicious plants on the way to the beach, about those strangers who knew more about her than they should, and about the whales and sharks gathering close to the shore. Telling Apothia was another way of telling Judd, minus the scrutinizing glare. But something held her back. Maybe because those things happened on the same night Nor had unintentionally healed Reed's cheek. She wasn't supposed to be able to do that. She wasn't sure what Judd or Apothia would do with that information. Practicing magic outside a witch's own Burden was black magic. It was . . . well, it was what her mother was doing. If they knew what Nor could do — *all* that she could do — wouldn't they look at her and see another Fern? How could they not? No, it was probably better for Nor not to say anything about that night at all.

Nor wasn't scheduled to work that morning, but she decided to stop by the Witching Hour after breakfast anyway. If, along the way, she saw the ocean looking like its usual self — specifically without a crowd of bizarrely behaving sea creatures — she might be reassured that the world wasn't falling to pieces.

What she saw, however, was hardly a comfort. Overnight, an invasive vine had taken over the hillside behind the Tower, smothering the lupines that normally blanketed the ground. And while the deciduous trees on the island typically enjoyed shedding their foliage at this time of year, today they waved their naked limbs forlornly. Nor hurried by, troubled by the melancholy that pulsed like a feeble heartbeat from their branches.

Nor entered the Witching Hour and found Vega sitting cross-legged on the floor in the corner of the shop, meticulously stacking copies of *The Price Guide to the Occult* in another new display.

Though it was cold, the sun shone brightly through crystal prisms hanging in the windows, casting tiny rainbows across the black pentacle painted on the floor and across the shoes of customers waiting in line at the register. The first in line was, strangely, Bliss Sweeney.

She hardly ever comes in here, Nor thought warily.

Nor shot an exasperated — and pointless — look toward Vega, who was oblivious to the impatient customers, and then stepped behind the counter to ring up Bliss's items.

As she was doing this, she became aware of Bliss studying her. Nor stole a quick glance at her face. It was pinched, hollow. There wasn't anything particularly different about the way Bliss looked, but she seemed — pained somehow.

Bliss suddenly grabbed Nor's hand, demanding her attention. The movement was quick and unexpected, reminiscent of the way an abused animal might attack without provocation. "You really don't look anything like her," she blurted.

Nor didn't need to ask who Bliss meant. The tattoo on her wrist said it all.

It was a fern, the tip curled like the end of a violin. Everyone in the shop was a Fern Follower; every single one of them had a freshly inked fern — most still red and raised — scrawled across an exposed shoulder blade or collarbone, or on a wrist or throat.

Nor had been eight when Fern had given herself her first tattoo. Nor had woken up in the middle of the night to find Fern sitting on the edge of the mattress, an open safety pin between her fingers. Nor had watched her mother dip the needle into the green ink of a broken ballpoint pen. Then she had punctured the tender skin on the inside of her wrist over and over again, until she had had a crude fern drawn there.

"What do you think, Nor?" she had asked, and held up her wrist for Nor's inspection. She'd smiled wickedly as the impossible happened: the fern tattoo had come to life and begun inching its way across Fern's skin toward Nor.

Nor had scrambled backward as fast as she could, her sweaty palms and feet slipping on the nylon sleeping bag. With her back pressed up against the wall, she had whimpered as the fern bared spines and thorns like teeth. "Why is it doing that?"

"Because I want it to," Fern had said, her eyes narrowing. But then the tattoo had retreated, recoiled like a tongue back to Fern's wrist. Fern had examined the blood on her arm with interest. "And I always get what I want."

That wasn't exactly true. There would always be one thing Fern wanted that she couldn't have, and that was for Quinn Sweeney to love her.

Bliss pulled out a copy of *The Price Guide to the Occult* and opened the book to a tabbed page. "I sent in my order form just like it says you're supposed to, but I was refused." Bliss paused and licked her dry lips. "I thought maybe there was a chance that *you* could help me. I haven't heard from him in years, Nor," she said desperately. "My son. It's been seven years since he disappeared. I just need to know what happened."

Nor swallowed hard. "I can't —" she started.

Bliss began digging frantically in her purse. "I have money," she said. "I can pay you."

"It's not about money," Nor said. "I'm sorry, Bliss. I can't help you."

"You're her daughter," she said, crestfallen. "Can't you put in a good word for me?"

Nor shook her head. "I haven't spoken to my mother in years."

Bliss looked confused. "Oh," she said. "I thought I saw her —" She stopped, and Nor caught a glimpse of the look she shared with Vega. He shook his head, and Bliss said, "I must have been mistaken."

She hurried from the shop, and Nor turned sharply to Vega, still stacking copies of *The Price Guide to the Occult* with creepy reverence. "What was that look you gave Bliss?" she asked. "You haven't seen my mother, have you?"

"No, of course not," Vega replied phlegmatically.

As he spoke, a puff of purple vapor passed through his lips. Nor followed it with her eyes as it moved through the air like a poison before sticking to the window. Vega was lying. Sliding down the glass, his lie turned black and slick, bringing to mind mud and grease and bird shit.

Vega turned his head, the wooden beads he had threaded through his dreadlocked hair click-clacking together, and Nor spotted a green tendril inked into the umber-colored skin on the back of his neck. "No one has seen your mother on this island in years," Vega replied coolly. And this time, he was telling the truth.

Nor left the shop without another word, eager to escape those ominous fern tattoos. She plopped down on the bottom step, not caring that the rain had picked up again or that the biting cold ate its way through her loose-knit sweater or even that what was left of yesterday's eyeliner was smeared. She raised her face to the sky and closed her eyes. The rain cooled her cheeks. If only the rain could wash away everything else as well — the horrible sick feeling in her stomach, those green tattoos and purple clouds, and, most of all, her mother. More than anything, she wished she could find a way to sever her mother's noxious grip on people, tightening like a noose with every passing day. She opened her eyes, but instead of finding a world clear of Fern Blackburn, she found Reed Oliveira staring at her.

"You know it's raining, right?" he asked.

"Is it?" She tugged the sleeves of her sweater over her hands out of habit. "I hadn't noticed." His presence made her feel a little bit better. Thankfully, the only tattoo he had was that blackbird inked on his arm. "What are you doing here?"

He held up a paper bag. "Madge never picked up her order this week. For all we know, she could be dangerously low on peppermint and clary sage."

"That *would* be a disaster. You are an unsung hero. Don't let anyone ever tell you otherwise."

Reed laughed. "I was going to go for a run after I dropped this off. What do you say about joining me?"

"Are you sure you'll be able to keep up?"

"No," he said. "But I am damn well gonna try."

He gave Nor a silly grin that made her feel light-headed, and at that moment, despite everything else that was happening, she swore if Reed Oliveira asked her to build a ladder to the moon, she'd say yes.

"I'll have to go home to change first," she said.

She stood, and her sweater fell from one shoulder. Her

face flushed with pleasure when Reed's eyes settled on her bare skin. Then he frowned upon seeing the neat scars that lined her collarbone. She quickly pulled her sweater back into place, and her face flushed for a whole different reason. This was what it felt like to be around him — constantly pulled in two directions, wanting to be both seen and unseen, and not knowing which one she preferred.

A few minutes later, Nor left Reed waiting in the foyer of the Tower with Bijou while she ran upstairs to change. *Reed Oliveira is waiting for me*, she thought, her heart pounding as she threw on a pair of running tights, a clean sports bra, and a thick hoodie — all black, of course — jamming her thumbs into the holes she'd sliced into the cuffs to hide her wrists. She twisted her damp hair into a knot on the top of her head and grabbed her running shoes. At the bottom of the stairs, just for a second, she was certain she'd only imagined that he was there, in her house, waiting to go on a run with her. She was certain that she'd find only Bijou and her own delusion chasing each other around the kitchen. *Please still be there*, she thought, taking a moment to compose herself before she rounded the last few steps, just in case.

And he was, smiling that gorgeous smile of his with Bijou wiggling happily in his arms. Bijou had decided he liked Reed. Reed reminded him of sunshine.

Soon, Nor and Reed were running along the trail surrounding Celestial Lake. Antiquity trotted behind them, disgruntled.

For a while, they ran without talking. Nor tried to think of something to say, but thoughts came to her only in fragments, and none were worth saying aloud. Instead, she increased her speed, rounding the ridge on the side of the lake with quick strides, pleased — not to mention impressed — to find Reed pulling up beside her.

The only sounds were Antiquity's heavy panting, the splash of Reed's and Nor's steps on the wet trail, and the roar of the waterfall at the far end of the lake.

The woods up here are quiet, Nor noted. Strangely so. It wasn't until they crested the hill that Nor realized that the quiet was too complete. They hadn't seen any wildlife since a pair of chipmunks had followed them for a short time, chittering, "Run! Run!" To Nor, it had sounded less like a cheer and more like a warning, a warning that Nor tried to tune out.

They stopped in the mist of the waterfall to catch their breath. More wide than tall, Lilting Falls dropped a mere twenty-five feet, skipping down a stairstepped cliff. The pattern the falling water made on the rocks was delicate, like the gossamer grace of a lace curtain or a bride's wedding veil.

Antiquity, panting loudly, sank into a wet patch of moss by the side of the trail. Nor picked up a stone and rolled it around in her palm. It was an agate, the color of honey and smooth to the touch, like the round marble clutched in the tiny crow's claw she had tucked in her sweatshirt pocket. Nor tossed the stone into the lake.

She allowed her eyes to fall on the tattoo on Reed's arm. Every time he moved, the blackbird seemed to fly. He smiled at her. Following her gaze, his smile turned sheepish.

"I never noticed other people's tattoos until I got one myself," he mused, leaning closer so that she could hear him over the roar of the falls. "Lately, I've seen a bunch of people on the island with the same tattoo, some kind of plant or something." He met her eyes. "Have you noticed? I wonder what the story is behind that."

"Does there have to be some deep rationale behind every tattoo?" she asked, trying to mask her sudden anxiety. The last thing Nor wanted to think about right now was her mother.

"Not necessarily, but don't say that to all those sorority girls with their matching infinity signs. It would break their hearts."

Nor laughed. "Well, I don't think I've ever seen a blackbird tattoo before. So two points for originality."

"Not if you consider the reason I got it." Reed smiled at her guiltily. "It was after a breakup."

"Oh, shit." Nor shook her head, embarrassed by the wave of jealousy that surged in her chest. She matched his grin with her own. "So your tattoo *does* have one of those deep but clichéd rationales! There's a story here, isn't there?"

Reed stared out at the water for a long time, thinking. Finally, he ducked his head and let out a half sigh, half laugh. "Fuck it," he said, "you win. Yeah, there's a story."

"And?" she prompted.

"And —" He sighed and ran his hands over his face. "The problem was I wasn't the only one she'd ensnared. I was just the one stupid enough to stay caught for as long as I did." He picked up a rock and flung it into the lake as hard as he could. It landed with an angry plop.

He sat on a fallen tree trunk on the side of the trail. Nor sat, too, feeling the spray of the waterfall on her cheeks. The log was nothing but a husk now, but she could still make out a hint of its spicy fragrance. She scraped her fingers across the red bark, and in doing so, disturbed a yellow jacket hiding in a knot in the wood. It buzzed at her, angry, until Nor waved it away.

Reed squeezed his hand into a fist, and the bird's black wings seemed to flutter. "After I ended it, I realized I just wanted to be back home. My last stop before leaving the mainland was a tattoo shop." He turned away from the water and looked at Nor. "The idea was that this way, whenever I thought about her, I'd look down at my tattoo and remember —"

"The hot searing pain of having a needle punctured into your skin a hundred thousand times."

Reed laughed, embarrassed. "Something like that."

"So that's it?" Nor asked, laughing. "It's just going to be you and your bird tattoo all alone on Anathema Island for the rest of your life, huh?"

Reed nodded, feigning seriousness. "Damn right it is. I

was thinking I could get into stamp collecting to pass the time. Maybe get some reptiles."

"Like snakes?"

"Really deadly ones," he said. "And iguanas. A couple Gila monsters. Anything to solidify my reputation as the island's resident reptile man. We don't have one of those yet."

Nor laughed. "Sounds like you have it all figured out."

"I thought I did, but I don't think I'm going to be able to think about pain every time I look at my arm anymore."

"No?"

"No. I'll be too busy thinking about you and how hard you laughed at my dumb bird tattoo." He smiled, and Nor's cheeks were aching from laughing so much. "How could I think about you and be in pain?" he said. "You aren't pain. Even the bees don't sting you."

You don't know that. Nor thought about the scars that covered her skin, scars from a time when it had seemed like pain was the only thing that kept her tethered to the ground. Would she ever be able to forget that pain?

Reed leaned toward her, so close that she could see the droplets of water on his skin and on his eyelashes. They reminded her of morning dew on a blade of grass or a flower petal. Nor's heart skipped a beat. *Oh shit, he's going to kiss me.* But before she could even decide whether she wanted him to kiss her — rather, whether she wanted to *let herself* want him to kiss her — he didn't.

Reed got up, strolled over to Antiquity, and scratched

her gently behind the ears. Nor cringed, certain Antiquity would find the gesture condescending, but as much as she didn't want to like him, the old dog couldn't seem to help herself.

"Come on. I'll race you home," Reed said, and took off down the trail. Antiquity was quick to pull herself to her feet and sprint after him.

First Bijou, Nor thought as she started down the trail. *And now Antiquity?* If Reed somehow found a way to win over Judd, too, she'd be screwed.

Nor let Reed take the lead for most of the run back, leaving herself space to obsess unhealthily about how, a few moments ago, she had been certain that Reed wanted to kiss her.

They rounded Meandering Lane and passed the dock just as the ferry pulled away. Its few passengers stood on the deck. Nor suspected each of them had their own nefarious green tattoo.

Nor shivered. Her mother hadn't shown any interest in her or the island since she'd left. The fear of Fern's return may have been a dark cloud that hung over Nor's head, but it was still a cloud, which was a far easier thing to fear than the possibility of having to face the real life thing itself — especially if the real thing was Fern Blackburn.

Nor traced the raised lines on her wrist with her thumb. Those had been Nor's first scars. The ones her mother had given her when she'd split open Nor's wrists and elbows and spilled her own child's blood across the roof. The rest of Nor's scars she had done to herself. After she'd received her Burdens, she could barely look at herself in the mirror without feeling afraid. She'd carved that pain into her skin using whatever sharp object she could find — a razor, a pair of scissors, or the sharp point of a pin. Now, when she ran her hands over her arms and legs, the skin there still read like braille, relating the story of how, for reasons even Nor couldn't understand, hurting herself had once been the only thing that made her feel better.

Nor glanced over at Reed. The rain slipping down his face. His hands white with cold.

It's better that he didn't kiss me, she decided, certain that if Reed Oliveira ever got close enough to learn all her terrible secrets, there would be no denying that pain might in fact be all Nor knew.

8

Revelation Spell

*"One should only search for a truth
that is impossible to find."*
— Rona Blackburn

Nor wove her way through the piles of abandoned junk that made up the Society for the Protection of Discarded Things. A wintry rain pattered gently on the roof.

She picked up a book on aphids with one hand and a mystery novel about a murder on a train with the other. "Savvy, what section am I in?"

"Green," Savvy answered from her perch on a director's chair near the front counter. With a red scarf tied expertly around her plum-colored pin curls and an old jumpsuit from her dad's mechanic shop hanging off her petite frame, Savvy looked a bit like a punk rock Rosie the Riveter.

The Society served as a glorified scrapyard, and it looked the part: piles of junk sat atop other piles of junk, some in towering configurations even Savvy had to marvel at from time to time. Almost anything could be found here — used appliances, water skis, a full set of silver cutlery. And if something was lost, it was always the first place to look. Savvy once claimed she had found a nun's habit, a pair of red clogs, and an abandoned engagement ring (minus the diamond), all while digging through a day's worth of deserted items.

"Green?" Nor put the two books — noting they both had green covers — off to the side and grabbed a dog-eared paperback from one of the other shelves. After glancing at the lustful couple on the cover, she tossed it to Savvy. "I found that book you didn't know you were looking for."

"Damn." Savvy examined the lewd cover. "Well, you know what they say. The best time to find something is when you're not looking for it. A couple of weeks ago, Heckel Abernathy wandered in and found some old matchbox car he had as a kid — *the very same one* — and he swore he'd lost that thing like seventy-five years ago."

"He's not that old."

Savvy rolled her eyes. "Well, then, *fifty* years ago. Anyway, the point is that if shit gets lost on this island, it always ends up here. That's science."

"That's — what?" Nor laughed. "No, that's not science, Savvy. That has nothing to do with science."

"Believe what you want. This book is a keeper, and you

know it." She wedged the book into her backpack. Sighing softly, Bijou shifted in his sleep, his body curled into an impossibly small circle of fluff at her feet.

Behind them, two girls sorted through a rack of vintage clothes. A man carrying a long hose of copper tubing over his shoulder searched a box of spare appliance parts.

To say the Society for the Protection of Discarded Things was a bit slow this morning would have been an understatement; all the shops along Meandering Lane seemed to be suffering from the same problem. Madge had even suspended the Witching Hour's walking tours. Nor had first assumed it was just the time of year or that maybe one of the ferries was out, but as more time passed, the less likely either of those seemed. With each passing day, fewer and fewer people were on the island. She recalled what Savvy had said about how dogs could sense an earthquake even before the ground started to shake. To Nor, it felt eerily similar to the way the ocean receded before a tsunami hit. Or how the birds flew away before the forest burst into flames.

On her morning run that day, even the ground, covered in a typical early December frost, had set her teeth on edge. Nor had tried to focus on normalcy: her arms pumping at her sides, breath turning to clouds in the cold, heart beating, feet pounding down the trail around Celestial Lake, the rhythmic panting of Antiquity at her side. Still, she hadn't been able to shake a feeling of doom. Her head had felt strangely empty without those squirrels and chipmunks twittering at her from the trees. Near Lilting Falls, she'd seen a cluster of oak trees with nettles wrapped around their trunks, covering them completely. It was as if they were prepared for battle, dressed in the armor of stinging leaves. A peculiar fog had settled over the ocean, just a couple of miles offshore. To Nor, it had looked as if those opaque clouds had swallowed the rest of the archipelago whole.

Nor absentmindedly pulled the crow's claw Reed had gotten her for her birthday out of her pocket. It wasn't particularly pretty — it was certainly a bit macabre. She thought the opaque gemstone could have been an opal; it was hard to tell. It was cloudy and dull and most of it blackened, almost as if from flames. Only when she held it up to the light could she see the tiniest bit of purple peeking through. Still, if it was an opal, then Nor could see why opals had once been called "eye stones": it made her feel as though there were something staring back at her.

"Oh, that reminds me. I've got something for you," Savvy said, hopping off the chair. It fell to the ground with a clatter, and Bijou scurried away. Savvy marched past Nor in her leopard-print platform shoes, calling "We're closed now!" over her shoulder.

"I like to keep obscure hours," she explained to Nor after the few customers had left. "It adds to the mystique of the place. Ambience is everything, you know."

Nor followed Savvy down the narrow aisles, past toppling piles of timeworn quilts and yellow-stained lace curtains.

"Hey! Be mindful of my crap!" Savvy scolded when Nor knocked over a pair of hedge trimmers.

Savvy stopped at a glass display case and pulled out a tarnished silver tray bearing a sign written in Savvy's handwriting: TREASURE TROVE. The tray held various odds and ends that only Savvy could consider precious, like several bullet casings, a crystal from a chandelier, a necklace that looked like a snake, and a long silver chain. Savvy plucked the tiny crow's claw out of Nor's hand, and before Nor could say a word, slid the trinket along the silver chain and fastened it around Nor's neck.

"There," she said, stepping back and examining her work. "Now the next time you see Reed, he'll think you actually like his gift. Even though it's weird as hell."

Ever since their run—the one that had ended with Reed not kissing her—Nor had pretty much done everything she could to avoid him. She hadn't responded to the text message he'd sent her last week. She didn't answer when he called a few days after that. Sure, it was partly out of sheer humiliation, but it was also in his best interest: if Reed was determined to stay away from pain, then it wouldn't do him any good to get entangled with her.

Outside, the rain began to beat against the windows,

shaking the panes of glass in their flimsy frames. Through the rain and the Society's open barn door, Nor glanced at the Witching Hour, relieved that the windows were too fogged up to see through. Earlier in the week, Nor had walked in on a discussion Vega and Madge were having in the shop. Based on the way Madge had been gripping Vega's arm, Nor assumed it was some kind of disagreement. There was something unsettling, almost brutish, about how Madge had smiled at Nor when she saw her: her lips pulled too taut, her teeth bared. Her motions had seemed newly felid; Nor almost expected to look down at her hands and see claws, to see fangs, not teeth, in her mouth. There were beads of sweat on Vega's trembling upper lip. When Madge had turned, Nor spotted the fronds of a fern peeking out from over the top of her T-shirt. The green tattoo made her warm beige skin look sickly.

The scene had reminded Nor too much of how they used to be before Fern had left the island, when Vega and Madge and all the rest were at Fern's beck and call. Even then, however, she'd never seen anything in them that resembled cruelty or fear.

Nor was certain the disagreement was somehow linked to those fern tattoos. Lately, it felt like everywhere she looked, another person had one. She'd noticed Bliss Sweeney's first, of course. Then Vega and Wintersweet and Madge. Now they seemed to be all over the country. Talk show hosts, television stars, and even some religious leaders — all had green ferns scrawled across their skin in worshipful mimicry of their new deity, Fern Blackburn.

Nor saw her former classmate Catriona dash across the street and find refuge from the rain in the Witching Hour. Nor was certain that underneath that new size-two winter coat, Catriona's skin was covered in coiling green tattoos.

"Your mom has fans everywhere these days," Savvy mused. "Did you hear she met with the president last week?"

Nor nodded. Fern's popularity had apparently earned her an invitation to the White House. There were pictures of her mother and the president all over the Internet. When Nor looked closely enough, she'd seen that, sure enough, their country's leader had a new fern tattoo on her arm.

"Your mom is amazing," Savvy continued, "but also kind of terrifying, in an evil-queen kind of way. I can totally imagine her convincing the huntsman to kill me so that she can eat my heart, you know?"

Nor did know. Her mother was like a perpetual stink in the air, a dull ache in the back of her head, the incessant beat of a snare drum. Nor wondered if the ominous events on Anathema were connected to a sense she had that her mother was drawing closer with each passing day. When she peered out into the rain, she almost expected to see her lurking out there in the gloom, almost expected to see everything the way it had been the last time Fern was here: flames shooting from the Witching Hour's roof, those too-bright stars in the sky, blood pouring from Nor's wrists and elbows.

Nor ran her fingers over her scars. Time might heal all wounds, but what about the scars those wounds left behind? Even if Nor's physical scars faded away, she would always remember where they had been, always be able to trace the path of her pain with her fingertips.

Nor moved away from the door.

"These spells that your mom's selling," Savvy said cautiously, "she really can cast them?"

Nor sighed. "Yeah, I guess she can," she admitted. "But, Savvy, I don't think the Resurrection Spell is something —"

"I'm not asking about that," Savvy interrupted. "I'm just wondering, if she can cast spells, who's to say that you might not be able to do the same?"

"I'm sure I can't," Nor answered quickly.

"But you're still a witch, right?"

Nor balked, nearly tripping over a pair of snakeskin boots. "I'm a — what?"

Savvy rolled her eyes. "Come on, Nor. You're a witch or, well, you're a *something*."

Nor opened her mouth to deny it, and then she looked at Savvy, really looked at her. This was her best friend. Suddenly, Nor didn't know how she'd managed to wait this long to tell her. "How long have you known?" Nor finally asked.

"A few days short of forever." Savvy was so matter-of-fact

that Nor couldn't help but laugh. "It's like I told you," Savvy said. "I'm nosy. I notice shit, like you always know when the weather's going to change. And the whales on your birthday? You seemed to know what they were thinking. Plus," she added quietly, "you knew my mom was going to die before anyone else did. I could see it in your face."

Nor opened her mouth and then closed it. She wasn't sure what to say to that. "Why haven't you ever said anything?" she finally asked.

Savvy shrugged. "I figured you didn't want to talk about it. I mean, let's face it, Nor. You don't want to talk about most things. Though" — Savvy examined Nor with a careful eye — "now that you *are* talking, I have some questions."

Nor sighed. "Yeah, that makes sense. Go ahead then."

Savvy settled onto a mint-green settee and folded her arms comfortably behind her head. "Are you immortal?" she asked.

Nor smiled. "I don't think immortality is possible, even in the magic world. Though my grandmother's dog is over one-hundred-sixty years old, so I could be wrong."

"What about him?" Savvy pointed to Bijou, who was busy trying to coax a mouse out from behind an old jukebox. "He isn't immortal or hundreds of years old, is he?"

"No," Nor answered, "and Bijou doesn't want to be immortal, either."

"How do you know that?"

"I can read his thoughts."

"Interesting. Can you read mine?"

"No."

"Why his?"

"I can only read the thoughts of animals — birds, squirrels, dogs. And plants," Nor added.

"Plants have thoughts?"

"Yes."

"What's that plant thinking?" Savvy asked, pointing to a potted geranium on the windowsill.

"That it's not a rose, and it wishes you'd stop referring to it as one."

"No shit? But you can't cast spells? Isn't that what witches do?"

Nor shook her head. "Not necessarily. Casting spells is just one skill out of many that a witch can have. No one in my family has been able to cast even a simple memory charm since my great-great-great-great-great-great-grandmother Rona Blackburn." Nor did the best she could to explain everything she knew about Rona and the curse that had befallen all the Blackburn daughters after her.

"So you're not just a witch, you're a cursed witch." Savvy considered this. "That's totally fucked up."

"That's not even the worst part." Nor sighed. "For generations, Blackburn women have been given one talent — incredible strength, speed, the ability to walk through fire, or heal pain through touch. My mother is casting spells she shouldn't be able to cast. Practicing magic outside a

123

witch's natural abilities isn't just frowned upon. It's black magic. It's considered wicked and evil because you have to do wicked and evil things in order to do it."

"Like what?"

"You have to be willing to hurt someone," Nor said softly. "Even kill them. Some witches have gone so far as to hurt their own children to get what they want." *The night sky bright with fire. The charred black of burned skin. Pools of blood.* "Trust me when I say the price paid for one of my mother's spells isn't just monetary. The real price is blood. And pain."

Which is why Nor had never told anyone that being able to communicate with nature — her most innocuous gift — was only one of many abilities she'd been given. Every time Nor accidentally stopped time or healed pain or saw a lie, she was afraid. Afraid that if people knew, they'd look at Nor and see someone evil and wicked, afraid they'd look at Nor and see Fern.

"So you're saying on a scale of one to ten, the likelihood of you casting, I don't know, a *love spell* is, what do you think, a four?"

"More like negative eleven. And love spells don't actually make anyone fall in love with you. It just mimics the physical responses to the feeling of being in love."

"So like sweaty palms and a racing pulse?"

"Pretty much."

"Gross."

Nor laughed. Of course, in some hands, a love spell could cause far more damage than an increased heart rate. A love spell could take away a person's autonomy. They'd love you because they'd have to love you. They wouldn't have any other choice. Nor thought about her father. Part of Nor knew Quinn Sweeney was still alive, that he was still under Fern's control. What could such a spell do to someone long-term? Was there anything left of him, or was he just a shell of who he once was? "I guess we're lucky that you don't want a love spell then, huh?" she finally said.

"I might not, but you could sure use one," Savvy said.

"My love life isn't really my top concern right now."

"Yes, it is!" Savvy insisted. "Whether or not your mom is a sociopath in witch's clothing, you still totally want to get underneath Reed. Hell, girl, I'd even settle for you to hook up with what's-his-name, that hot angry guy on the beach."

"Gage Coldwater?" Nor exclaimed. "You can't be serious. He's hated me since seventh grade!"

"Which could be fun," Savvy posited. "Nor, you care about Reed. And maybe you don't want to admit it because then you'll have to consider what happens if it doesn't work out. You and I both know that losing someone hurts like hell, but that's how you know that it meant something. That it was real. Isn't that worth it?"

Nor glanced at the raised skin in the crook of her elbow. She could hear the scars on her arm calling to her, and she could feel that familiar ache — the ache to stop caring, to mask it with blood and pain. She tugged down her sleeve and clasped her hand over her singing scars. Savvy was right. Nor did care about Reed. In fact, she cared so much that she sometimes felt it would swallow her whole. But that was the whole point. She cared about him enough to stay away.

"Okay, new plan," Savvy decided. "I may not know anything about curses or psycho moms, but as your best friend, I promise that I *will* help you get it on with whomever you want. Reed or what's-his-name or Heckel Abernathy if that's your kink. On the condition that, *should* any of this manifest, you have to give me all the delicious details. Deal?"

Nor smiled, and then followed Savvy and Bijou out of the chaos of the Society for the Protection of Discarded Things — past toppling towers of scorched pots and pans, a scattering of broken-down lawn mowers, and an antique metal dress form. Though Savvy couldn't actually solve the bulk of Nor's problems, Nor felt better having been reminded that someone gave enough of a shit to try.

Around this time of year, Meandering Lane was usually ablaze with strands of tiny twinkling white lights draped across trees and strung along rooftops. There would be mistletoe and holly greens hanging above the front door of the Witching Hour, and Heckel Abernathy would have fixed the eight gaudy reindeer atop the Willowbark General Store. There would be a wooden nativity scene in front of the library and a menorah flickering from the front windows of Harper Forgette's and Reuben Finch's houses. A medley of secular Christmas carols would be blaring from the ferry speakers. But this year only a single strand of red and green lights hung limply from the front door of the co-op.

"The holiday spirit is hard to find around here this year," Savvy said.

Though it was no longer raining, the air felt cold and wet against Nor's face. She scooped up Bijou and wiped his muddy paws with her mittened hand before bundling him inside her jacket.

The heat from the ovens had steamed up the Sweet and Savory Bakery windows, but she could still see the blurred outline of Bliss Sweeney, preparing marzipan scones or maybe a batch of cranberry-orange biscotti — both favorites during this time of year — in the hopes of attracting some scant customers. Through the opaque glass, Bliss looked like a colorful ghost.

With heavy steps, Nor followed Savvy toward the Witching Hour. She knew she should check in on Madge, but she was afraid of what she'd find — which was why she'd brought Savvy with her.

They passed Catriona on the stairs. She avoided their eyes, ignored Savvy's cheerful hello, and practically fell over the railing in her haste to get away from them.

"Is it just me," Savvy said, "or have cartoon villains looked less suspicious than she did just then? I bet she stole something like —" Savvy suddenly stopped. Her mouth agape, she pointed as that peculiar fog Nor had seen on her run that morning suddenly billowed in from the ocean. It quickly spread across Meandering Lane. From the top of the stairs, they watched as, little by little, the entire island seemed to vanish. First Willowbark and then the library; soon, Nor could barely make out the strand of lights hanging from the front door of the Artist Co-Op. She looked up at the Witching Hour. The fog had hidden the shop from sight.

Almost like camouflage, Nor thought.

"What is this?" Savvy said, shaking the fog out of her burgundy curls. "A sign of the end of times? Should I be freaking out right now?"

"I don't think so." Nor swept her hand through the mist, and it swirled around her fingers like cotton candy. "I think it's just — fog." Nevertheless, it was unlike any fog that Nor had ever seen.

They stumbled up the stairs, and Nor held her breath when they opened the front door. The shop, like the street, was empty. Nor's and Savvy's steps echoed eerily.

A few seconds passed, and then Madge pushed through the back doorway. She stopped abruptly. The curtain clung to her shoulder, and she gave the room behind her a furtive glance before she said to Nor, "I didn't schedule you for today, did I?"

A wave of nostalgia washed over Nor. She had the sudden urge to embrace Madge, to rest her chin on her shoulder, and to breathe in the comforting aroma of Madge's vanilla-scented soap. Even from here, however, Nor could tell that something different wafted from Madge's skin now: a metallic smell, like a butcher shop at the end of the day. There were purple bags under her eyes, too, and gray strands in her straight black hair. Madge busied herself behind the cash register, and Nor could see fresh tattoos, red and raised and angry, spiraling up and down her arms and across her hands.

Out of curiosity, Nor pushed back the curtain and peeked into the back room. The room was dimly lit, the shades from all the windows drawn, and Wintersweet lay on a sofa pushed against the wall. Tattoos of Fern's malicious plant — more than Nor had ever seen — crawled across her golden-brown skin. They crept across the tops of her feet and wrapped around her ears; they covered her hands and curled down her fingers. Her breathing was ragged.

"What the hell happened to her?" Savvy said with a gasp, peering around Nor's shoulder.

A dark cloud passed over Madge's face, and the glance she cast in Wintersweet's direction seemed more culpable than caring. "She's just tired," she said, but a tremor was in her voice, and a greasy and glistening purple cloud floated out of her mouth and across the room. It splattered like a boil across a display of scented candles.

"If she's just tired," Savvy whispered, "then 'Sleeping Beauty' is definitely a horror story."

Nor nodded. There was nothing serene or restful about

the way Wintersweet looked. No, something had happened to her, just like something had happened to cause the sea-creature exodus from the Salish Sea, the empty forest, and those trees wearing stinging nettles like armor. Nor looked back at Wintersweet and then out at that fog creeping past the window. Her mind started to stray toward those sharp scissors hidden in the drawer below the cash register. It no longer seemed a question of *if* her mother would return to Anathema Island, but of *when*. And what in the hell was going to protect them when she did?

9

Divination Spell

"Do not wish for the gift of foresight.
It is a trite and greedy gift from which one shall surely
receive only disappointment."
— Rona Blackburn

Nor was dreaming. In her dream, she was standing at the edge of a precipice, overlooking miles of frothy gray ocean. She looked down and saw long, pointed nails, like talons, painted red. Green swirling tattoos covered her waxy skin.

Where am I? Something was familiar about this place. She'd been here before. Many times, in fact. Two people stood behind her, waiting. Something told her they would wait all day if she desired it. They would wait until their knees buckled, until they toppled over with hunger or their tongues dried up in their mouths.

Neither was much older than seventeen. One was a skinny punk who had so far proven to be about as noteworthy as his neglected Mohawk. The other was a slender girl Nor recognized as her former classmate Catriona. Both of their arms were covered in bandages. There was a gruesome gash on Mohawk's cheek.

Doubt was in Catriona's gaunt face, and Nor somehow knew that there could be no doubt today. Most especially from Catriona. That she was from the island was what made her useful, but if there was doubt —

She beckoned to Catriona, drew her close, and stroked her sunken cheeks with those red talons. The girl's thirst for her attention and approval flushed across her face like a fever.

"Not to worry, my pet," Nor purred in a voice not her own. "Do what I ask, and I promise, you will be rewarded immensely." Any doubt Catriona had felt was gone.

Nor watched as Mohawk boy and Catriona wended their way down to a small dinghy at the dock. Only a few abandoned boats remained in the marina, sticking out of the water like shattered teeth. The dinghy lurched into the gray. Soon, it was but a tiny pinpoint in the distance.

Nor turned her attention back to her surroundings. The crumbling roof of an abandoned building peeked out from over the treetops. There was a reason she was here. *What is it?*

Her mind filled with a memory that did not belong to her: the life draining from a man's eyes, blood pooling on the floor. She had been a bit overzealous with that one. And still, every drop of the man's blood had not been enough. It turned out he had been a stranger to the archipelago, so she could only cast but a few illicit spells with it before the feeble power of that sacrifice slipped through her fingers. This was why Catriona's compliance was so important — that couldn't happen again.

"At least killing him had been fun," Nor said aloud, and the voice that came out of her mouth chilled her to the bone.

It was then that Nor remembered why she was here. It had nothing to do with the place. The place was inconsequential — a convenient means to an end. No, this had everything to do with the people. The new hope for power raced through her veins like a drug. The true price of her spells had nothing to do with money. What did someone who could have anything she wanted need with money? No, the true price was blood. And pain. It was simple and somewhat trite, but it was also wicked, which was what made it so fun.

It didn't take long for the boat to return. At first, it appeared that they had failed, but as they disembarked and made their way up the trail, she saw they were dragging someone with them — a woman. Her head lolled sluggishly against her chest. Even from here, Nor could see the green vines inked into her skin.

"Is she dead?" she asked in the voice that was not her own.

"You said you wanted her alive," Catriona answered.

"And so I did."

Nor looked at the woman's face and frowned. She turned to the boy and slapped him hard across the face.

"But you said you wanted —" he cried.

"I was very clear about who I wanted."

"We — we couldn't get to her," he stammered, avoiding looking into her eyes. "She closed the bakery early. But this one's from the island. Isn't that enough?"

"No, it is not. Was I or was I not quite explicit about that detail?"

Mohawk and Catriona shared a look. "Should we take her back?" Catriona dared to ask.

Nor examined the woman, slumped over like a dumb beast raised for slaughter. She might not have been the one she had requested, but she wouldn't have to be wasted altogether.

"I suppose she'll do for now."

The two breathed a sigh of relief. Nor raised her arm, and the fern tattoo unlatched from her skin. Nor knew she could cause people pain just by thinking it, could split their skin open just by desiring it, but that wasn't quite as memorable and not nearly as nightmarish.

The fern wrapped itself around the woman's neck and made a deep puncture wound. The woman whimpered. The thorns the ferns sprouted were sharp, but not too sharp. Too sharp and they wouldn't hurt — not at first. Where was the fun in that?

The fern was readying itself to sink deeper into the woman's skin when Nor gave a jolt, and the fern retracted with a crack.

"What is it?" Catriona asked. "What's wrong?"

"Shut up!" Nor commanded, and listened harder. She swore someone, from quite a distance away, had started to scream.

Nor lurched awake, throwing her hands out in front of her as if to halt some disaster. The pale sky told her it was early morning. The cold January air seeped through the thin windowpanes. Her pillow lay on the floor on the other side of the room. Bijou inched his way back out from under the dresser, and Nor breathed a shaky sigh of relief. Her throat felt raw.

As if, she realized with a start, *I'd been screaming.*

The sound of footsteps pounding on the stairs sent Bijou back under Nor's dresser. Judd burst into the room wielding a large metal bat. Antiquity was close behind, ears pinned flat to her head, hackles raised in alarm.

"What in God's great green pastures was all that hollering for, girlie?" Judd thundered, dropping the bat to the floor. It landed with a clatter that sent Nor's pulse racing once more. Nor told herself that even though the dream had *felt* real, that didn't mean it *was* real. She'd had plenty of realistic dreams before — dreams in which she could fly or run on water. In one dream, all of her teeth had fallen out. She looked down at her nails. They were not painted red. Her skin was not covered in green spiraling tattoos.

"It was just a nightmare," Nor insisted, her words turning into a little purple cloud.

Judd pulled her pipe out of the breast pocket of her pajamas and stuck it between her teeth. "That's it?" she said, shaking her head. "All that noise over a bad dream?"

Nor just nodded, distracted by the purple cloud floating up to the skylight and plastering itself to the glass.

"Well, you're awake now," Judd said. "Apothia's got breakfast on the table if you're hungry." She paused and picked up the metal bat before leaving the room. Nor was suddenly worried that Judd could see her lie splattered against the window. But of course she couldn't.

Nor hugged her knees to her chest. *It wasn't just a nightmare*, she thought. *But what the hell was it?* Fern couldn't possibly be anywhere near them. Last time Nor had checked, her mother was on a national book tour. She'd read online that at one of her mother's New England events, several people had been hospitalized after waiting in line for over four hours in the middle of a snowstorm. Losing a few toes to frostbite was apparently a small price to pay for a chance to meet Fern Blackburn.

When Nor got downstairs, Judd was at the front door, speaking to an unfamiliar woman wearing a Pendleton scarf and an older man in a sweat-stained Stetson. "Sorry about this, Judd," the woman was saying. "You know I wouldn't have come here if I didn't think it was absolutely necessary."

The woman in the scarf turned, and two young men came into view behind her. It was Pike and Sena Crowe Coldwater. Nor recognized them from that night on the beach. They were carrying someone — an unconscious woman whose brunette hair was wet with blood.

Judd grunted and motioned them inside urgently. "Apothia!" she barked over her shoulder.

Without hesitation, Apothia grabbed hold of the table-cloth on the dining room table and sent the remnants of their breakfast crashing to the ground. Plates and coffee mugs shattered against the floor. A piece of buttered toast slid slowly down a wall along with splatters of orange juice and smears of jam.

The two young men laid the unconscious woman gently across the table. Judd rolled up her sleeves, her brow furrowed in concentration.

"We found her on the steps of the Witching Hour," Pike said. "Looks like she either stumbled into something, or —"

"More like something stumbled into her," the older man finished.

"This wound here is a nasty one," Judd muttered, examining a laceration across the back of the woman's head.

"I had my best people working on her," the woman in the scarf said, "but for the life of them, they could not get any results. I'm telling you, these injuries did not come from anything natural." She looked at Judd's hands, placed on either side of the wound. "How's her pain?"

"Whatever it was that got to her, Dauphine," Judd answered, "was meant to hurt. That I'm sure of."

Apothia brushed the woman's hair away from her face. It was Wintersweet.

Nor's palms began to sweat. She edged closer to the table, stepping on broken china and cold toast. Blood from the head wound stained Judd's hands. Familiar and gruesome lesions circled Wintersweet's neck.

As if made by barbed wire, Nor thought, *or a thorny vine.* Was it possible that the dream hadn't been a dream at all?

I don't want this, Nor thought, backing away from the table. If it was a premonition, why did it have to be *this* one? And why now? It wasn't fair. She wasn't even safe in her dreams.

"Standing there gaping is about as useful as a handkerchief with holes in it, girlie," Judd rumbled. "Get her out," she muttered to Apothia. "It's too damned crowded in here anyway."

Apothia put a hand on Nor's shoulder. "Let your grandmother work," she murmured.

Nor nodded dumbly and let Apothia steer her toward the back door.

She shoved her feet into the felt boots Apothia kept near the door and grabbed one of Judd's thick alpaca wool sweaters. Just before closing the door behind her, she saw Judd pull one of her hands away from the back of Wintersweet's head and hold it out to the woman she'd called Dauphine. Dauphine calmly pulled long silver quills from out of Judd's palm. As they emerged, they dissipated into thin air.

Outdoors, Nor felt a little better. She wrapped her grandmother's sweater more tightly around herself and was comforted by the scratchy wool against her skin. The sweater was so large it practically dragged on the ground, but it smelled like Judd: pipe tobacco and cayenne pepper and the sharp tang of antibacterial soap.

Bijou, who'd followed her outside, trotted off the path, drawn by a rustling in the rhododendron bushes. His little ears pricked up, and his thoughts filled with flashes of wild animals — raccoons, rabbits, and wild turkeys. He was desperately hoping for a turtle. Nor crouched down to peer into the brush with the little dog and then fell back with a start.

What they were looking at was definitely not a turtle.

Glowing yellow eyes in a narrow canine face stared back at them. The red fox quickly leaped over her and, with two silent bounds, was over the fence and into the thick of the forest.

Before he disappeared from view, Nor caught a few of the fox's thoughts. He was there to see *her*, not out of curiosity, but as if he'd been sent on a mission to check on her. What was stranger was that he was off to report that she was safe. *Why would someone need to know that?*

"He didn't seem to like you much," a voice said.

Nor jumped. "You scared the hell out of me," she yelped, glaring at the boy sitting on the porch of Apothia's little white studio. "What are you doing here?"

"I came with Dauphine and my cousins," Gage said coolly. He tipped his head back and took a long drag off a cigarette.

Nor had the intense desire to punch him in his smug face.

"Then why is everyone *else* who came with Dauphine inside helping," Nor asked spitefully, "while you're sitting out here in the cold?"

"Good point." He paused to take another long pull off his cigarette. "But then again, who else is out here with me?"

Well, he's not wrong. Nor watched the ash spill from the end of his cigarette before finally admitting, "To be honest, you probably know a lot more about what's going on than I do."

Gage studied her, then moved over and motioned for her to sit next to him. "What do you want to know?"

"You're going to tell me?" Nor was surprised.

"I'm feeling generous this morning, but who knows how long that'll last, so you better talk fast, kid."

I could probably get at least one good punch in. Probably. "Why do you —" Nor started, careful to keep a comfortable distance between herself and Gage when she sat down, "and a bunch of people I've never even met — seem to know so much about my family? Things no one else knows?"

"We really are starting at the beginning, aren't we?" Gage shook his head. "Well, that's because of an agreement made between my ancestors and the mighty matriarch of your family, Rona Blackburn."

"What kind of an agreement?" Nor asked.

"A binding one, apparently," he said sardonically. "Did you know it was my ancestors who put out the fire that almost destroyed the island? No, you've probably only been told about how your great-great grandmother bravely saved all those books from being burned to a crisp. And Astrid Blackburn didn't rebuild the whole island, not single-handedly at least. My family helped her, just like they've helped every Blackburn daughter, including Rona herself."

"What do you mean?"

"Where did you think Rona went after those bastards burned down her house?"

Nor mulled this over. "So your ancestors have been here since —"

"Since before yours," Gage said. "By the time the so-called Original Eight showed up, my great-great-great-great-great-great grandfather, Lachlan Coldwater, had already been here for almost five years. He was kind of a hermit, but he had a wife, Nellie. They had kids, and their kids had kids. And so on." Gage turned to look at her. "Do you get what I'm telling you, kid? Anathema Island doesn't have eight colonizing patriarchs, it has —"

"Nine," Nor finished.

"I was going to say one, but yeah, I guess you could say nine."

The ramifications of what he was saying slowly dawned on her. Not *eight* original men, but nine. *Nine.* Nor's heartbeat quickened with dread. "But you said your ancestors took Rona in," she hurried to say. "So why would she —" She stopped herself before she could say it.

Gage gave her a look. "I know what you're thinking. That's the big unanswered question, isn't it? No one's certain whether or not my family is included in old Rona's backfired curse. Every generation, the male descendants of my family hold their breath and wait to see if it's their turn to succumb to the charms of a witch."

Nor blushed. "You know about that?" she asked quietly.

"Of course."

"And those descendants would include —"

"Yours truly."

Of course. For a moment, Nor didn't know what to say. It did clear up a few things, such as —

"Is *that* why you didn't want to work with me on that science project in seventh grade?" she blurted out.

Gage stared at her and then snorted with laughter. "Fuck, I'd forgotten all about that." He shook his head. "Yeah, but I also thought you would have made a lousy partner."

"I didn't know you were slated for valedictorian," Nor shot back.

"No, that will be my cousin Charlie," he said scathingly.

"Look, kid, I don't have all the answers. We might be part of the curse. We might not be." He tossed his cigarette on the ground, stood, and started walking away. "All I know is I sure as hell don't want to be the one to find out."

"Trust me," Nor called after him. "It wouldn't exactly be a dream come true for me either!"

What a dick. But once he was gone, a different and more desperate feeling started to creep into the pit of her stomach. Though she hated to admit it, Nor sympathized with him. He was afraid, and she knew what it was to be afraid. She knew that fear hurt in a way that was hard to explain; it could make you say things you never thought yourself capable of saying, do things you never thought you were capable of doing.

Nor stared at the lights in the Tower. A moment passed, and then another, and her attention was drawn to his discarded cigarette, still smoldering.

Nor picked it up, studied the dying embers, and imagined pressing the lit end into the back of her hand. She thought about the white-hot pain invoking that familiar rush of adrenaline. How it would soon enough be replaced by a dull nothingness, both soothing and addictive, that she'd tried so hard to forget.

Nor dropped the cigarette and crushed it under her foot until all that was left was a scorched mark on the ground.

Nor walked back into the Tower holding Bijou. Reluctantly, she put him down; it felt better to have him in her arms, with his thoughts of rainwater and pelicans to calm her. She followed him through the kitchen and saw Pike and Sena Crowe standing in the foyer, stoic statues on either side of the woman Judd had called Dauphine. Each had a large knife slung on his hip.

"Oh, come now, Judd," Dauphine was saying. "You're being difficult for the sake of being difficult." Sitting at Dauphine's side was, peculiarly, a wolfhound, one as large and as old as Antiquity.

"I am doin' nothing of the sort," Judd grumbled. Judd's posture was rigid. Her mouth was the taut line of a person who disliked what she was hearing. Antiquity loomed beside her.

Nor wasn't sure she'd ever seen anyone argue with Judd before. Apothia and Judd could orchestrate a knockdown, drag-out fight with just eyebrow raises and flared nostrils; Apothia had a way of soothing Judd's wild temper, and it certainly hadn't ever been by matching Judd's rage with her own.

"If you're all so damned worried about it," the older gentleman wearing the cowboy hat interjected, "I don't see why you all can't just come stay with us. You'll be safe as houses up there." He moved his hand as he talked. He was holding a knife, and briefly, it was all Nor could see, watching the flashing blade as he wove it deftly between his fingers.

"Because there is protocol to follow, Everly —" Dauphine reminded him.

"Dauphine —" Everly scoffed.

"And protocol," Dauphine continued, "hardly calls for sequestering Blackburn women without irrefutable evidence that they are, in fact, in danger."

"Too right," Judd grumbled.

"I'd like to get back to the matter of the woman we found on the brink of death a few hours ago," Dauphine continued.

Nor's heart sank. "But she's okay now, right?" she interrupted. Everyone turned to look at her. Nor turned to her grandmother. "You were able to heal her?"

"It wasn't anything I couldn't fix," Judd rumbled. "So don't you worry about that, girlie."

Nor breathed a tiny sigh of relief. She could feel Dauphine studying her. There was something about her that made Nor wary of looking her in the eye, afraid that it would be just as blinding as staring into the headlights of an approaching car or straight into the blazing sun. The wolfhound at her side cast a lupine shadow like a menacing shroud. But unlike Antiquity, whose thoughts brimmed with memories of the hunter she had once been, this wolfhound's thoughts were calm, as placid as a dank forest floor.

"For the time being," Dauphine finally said, "I think we need to keep our focus on figuring out exactly what happened to Wintersweet. So far, there is nothing to support the idea that this has relevance only for the Blackburn daughters. We must assume that there may well exist a threat to us all."

As the room erupted into a boisterous debate, Nor caught a glimpse through a window of Gage, who'd come back and was standing in the yard, his back turned to her. His cigarette sent a lone spiral of smoke into the morning air. Suddenly she felt like she was standing on the edge of a dark cliff, with an irresistible urge to jump.

Memory Spell

"There are some things worth forgetting. The irony is
that it is often this very thing that is forgotten."
— Rona Blackburn

Nor sat in a rickety wicker chair in front of Apothia's
little dance studio. A chilly March breeze came up off the
water. Nor wrapped her sweater more tightly around herself. Across from her, Wintersweet set down a cup of tea.
Her hand trembled as she passed another to Nor, the teacup
rattling in its saucer. Nor leaped up to take it from her to
avoid adding this one to the shards of broken porcelain she'd
already had to sweep up. Wintersweet looked at Nor expectantly. Nor raised the teacup to her lips and took a polite sip
of the air inside.

Judd had done all she could for Wintersweet. Any
physical ailments Wintersweet had suffered that night two

months ago were healed. But there were some types of pain that Judd couldn't heal. Nor knew all too well that some pain would not be erased. Some pain demanded to be felt.

Wintersweet had never been particularly chatty to begin with, but now it was difficult to get her to say much of anything. There were gaps in her memory, too, as if someone had carved parts of her away. She'd often remember that to make a fried egg, she had to use a pan, but she would forget that the egg must also be cracked. Or — like today — she'd remember the ritual of serving tea but forget the part about making it first. A few days earlier, she'd remembered how to turn on the kitchen faucet but not how to turn it off.

Wintersweet seemed to prefer hanging around the Tower rather than at the Witching Hour. Nor didn't blame her; the last time Nor had visited the shop, it had felt almost sinister. The gargoyles hanging from the walls had seemed cold and menacing. And something was wrong with Madge. Her tattoos looked infected. Her cheeks were sagged and droopy, as if her skin were suddenly too big for her. She'd shrugged off Nor's concerns. Nor hadn't spoken with her since.

As for Fern, her rising success and popularity continued to seem unstoppable. She was doing seminars now, offering her fans new ways in which to behold her benevolent talents. A renowned publication had named Fern Blackburn Person of the Year. Soon, her face would be adorning every checkout counter and newspaper stand in the country. There were even rumors that she'd been invited to meet with several foreign diplomats, and the Chinese ambassador had been spotted sporting his own green fern tattoo.

But lately, there'd also been reports of people going missing after attending one of Fern Blackburn's events. People had been disappearing around Anathema Island as well. No one had seen Catriona in weeks, and just yesterday, the Sweet and Savory Bakery had been uncharacteristically closed. Vega was also gone, but at least that vanishing act had an explanation. The last Nor had heard, he'd reconnected with his old flame Lake somewhere in rural Texas. Wherever he was, Nor hoped he was in a place Fern would never think to look.

The few people Nor had seen on Meandering Lane were Pike and Sena Crowe, though judging from the knives they always had slung on their hips, they weren't there to shop. Fortunately, Gage was never with them. Every time Nor saw Gage, she was overcome with the feeling that she was on the cusp of some terrible disaster, like she was standing in the path of a hurricane. Gage Coldwater felt dangerous, the way a sharp metal object felt dangerous, and try as she might, Nor had never been very good at keeping herself away from those.

The weather had remained cold and gray; the whales had yet to return. The island was void of its usual surge of tourists. Retirees hadn't returned to air out their summer homes; their lawns grew more feral with every passing day. For the most part, those who remained stayed locked in their houses, sealing their doors and windows against whatever nameless ghost had brought this air of unease to their island home. The animals, too, had hidden themselves away. The dogwood trees along Meandering Lane were covered in a toxic residue that could burn the skin. The juniper bushes in front of the Witching Hour screamed whenever Nor was within hearing range.

Nor stood and walked out into the overgrown yard, leaving Wintersweet to enjoy her tea party on her own. She made a point to avoid a hostile-looking holly bush and chose instead to pass through what looked like a benign patch of narcissus. When she did, she felt something prick her skin, and when she looked, she saw a bead of blood well up on her ankle.

It seemed now even the daffodils had thorns.

It was hours later when Nor wended down the trail that led to the beach. Behind her, the Tower loomed against the setting sun, like a fortress in some medieval legend. The plants along the trail were just as vicious as ever, and when she emerged, her sleeves were torn, her hands scratched and smeared with blood. She'd almost lost her scarf to a mean-spirited rhododendron bush. If she'd trusted herself with a knife, she would have brought one to fight them off, but ever since that incident with the cigarette back in January, Nor could barely glance at even a paper clip without feeling on edge.

Once she reached the shore, she unzipped her jacket, and Bijou hopped to the ground. The little dog scurried gleefully ahead of her, kicking up rocky sand as he ran.

It was nothing special, this beach, but its many nooks and crannies and delightful sea treasures that washed up on shore — gelatinous jellyfish and bulbous bull kelp and the occasional sea star — had made it the perfect place for Nor's childhood adventures. And as Nor spotted a familiar figure walking toward her, she realized it was perfect for other things as well; when the beach grass glowed silver in the moonlight, Nor could imagine how easily felicitous lovers might find each other in the dark here.

"Are you looking for the whales, too?" Reed called. When he got closer, Nor could see the tip of his nose had turned pink from the cold. "I keep thinking that I just haven't looked closely enough," he said, "but it doesn't look like there's anything but a few fish out there."

Nor had stopped expecting the whales to return, mainly because it wasn't just the whales that had disappeared. It had been weeks since Nor had come across a young deer and her fawn while on her evening run or woken up to the crows tormenting Antiquity through the bedroom windows. All of the sea creatures were long gone; even the ones who made their homes there had left. There were no breaching porpoises, no barking sea lions, and no seabirds gliding overhead, calling to one another with their cackling cries. She suspected the whales had skipped over the archipelago on purpose, disturbing migration patterns in search of more welcoming waters.

"Quite a change from a few months ago, huh?" Reed continued. "Now it's almost like they'd come last fall to say their good-byes."

And maybe they were trying to convince us to leave, too, Nor thought. "They could just be running late," she offered lightly.

"Maybe we should wait out here for them a little longer then," Reed said, smiling. "Just in case."

Typically, most especially in the early stages of spring, with winter and all its shivery consorts still breathing down their necks, nights on the island required a jacket as well as a scarf, mittens, and sometimes even a warm wool hat. But every time Reed looked at her, Nor swore the heat of her cheeks could warm the oceans.

Nor sat on one of the fallen logs along the beach and watched Reed build a fire. As it roared to life, bright flickers of orange and red danced against the darkening night sky. Bijou settled happily on the warm coils of Nor's discarded scarf.

"I haven't seen you around much," Reed said.

Nor blushed. *Was that a nice way of calling me out for avoiding him these past few months?* "I'm sorry," she muttered lamely. "I've been — busy."

"Don't be sorry." Reed shrugged. "I've been increasing my mileage just in case you'll join me on a run again."

"Really?"

"No," he admitted. "That last run almost killed me."

"What?" Nor laughed. "You didn't seem to be struggling to keep up."

"I'll attribute that to adrenaline and bravado," Reed said. "I was trying to impress you."

His hand brushed against hers. Nor's breath caught when his fingertips grazed the scars on her wrist, peeking out from the cuff of her sweatshirt. Her first inclination was to pull her arm away, to run away as fast as she could. But she didn't.

He took her hand. "Can I ask if it ever helped?"

"It didn't," she finally admitted softly. "Not enough."

Not even on the days when she hadn't stopped at one cut or when she'd cut too deep. Like the time Apothia had found her in the bathroom, blood gushing through her clamped fingers. She remembered the desperate rasp in Apothia's voice when she'd screamed for Judd. She remembered how that pain had come out of her as an effluvium that burned Nor's lungs. Thanks to Judd's quick work, that cut hadn't left a scar.

But try as she might, Judd could do nothing about the pain Nor felt on the inside. So Apothia took her to someone who could. Three times a week, she took Nor into the city for her therapy appointments. It wasn't so bad. Most of the time, they'd stopped for a bowl of pho or clam chowder at Pike Place Market before heading home. They'd always brought home those little salted caramels that Judd pretended not to love. And eventually, Nor had gotten better.

She wasn't any less afraid than she'd been before; it was more that the desire to carve out the parts of herself that scared her had become easier to control.

The ocean waves lapped gently against the beach, picking up pebbles and ribbons of algae. The water glittered with the bioluminescence of tiny phytoplankton. Another unnatural occurrence, it being too early in the year for its appearance, but it felt like an otherworldly gift just for the two of them. As if a constellation of stars had plummeted from the heavens for their amusement alone.

"You up for a swim?" Nor asked suddenly.

"Are you out of your mind?" Reed groaned. "It's freezing out there."

"That's the fun part." Before she could lose her nerve, Nor jumped up and unzipped her sweatshirt. She dropped it and the rest of her clothes in a heap near the fading fire as she raced down the rocky beach and, feeling the satisfying weight of Reed's eyes on her, plunged into the ocean.

The icy water pulled the air out of her lungs and numbed her skin. It hurt but not in a bad way. Her voice suddenly rushed to the surface, and she was laughing so hard she was screaming.

"It's not that bad," she hollered between chattering teeth. "Come in."

Reed shook his head and remained seated, warm and dry on the log. "Sure," he called. "It looks downright tropical out there."

154

"Okay, it's freezing," she admitted. "But the water is so beautiful, it's easy to ignore."

"Beautiful things tend to have a distracting effect," Reed said.

A slow grin pulled at the corners of his mouth before he stood and took off his jacket, then stripped off his T-shirt and jeans. Nor diverted her eyes until he was immersed in the water. His golden-brown skin glowed in the moonlight.

Their treading feet startled a few herring out of the water. It was reassuring to see there was something in the sea besides the two of them. The small fish twinkled like blue fireflies against the night sky. Nor sliced her hands through the waves in a smoky turquoise streak. The marks on her arms stood out purple and impervious in the water.

She reached up and brushed her fingers against Reed's shivering lips. He dipped backward, and the glow of the plankton illuminated his head like a halo. "It's starting to feel a little warm to me," he said.

Nor laughed. "I'm pretty sure that's what hypothermia feels like."

They hurried back to shore, stumbling over the rocks and into each other in their haste to get away from the icy water. They got back to the fire, their clothes, and Bijou, asleep on Nor's scarf. Reed wrapped them both in his jacket. When he kissed her, Nor could taste the ocean on his lips.

* * *

When they got back to the Tower, it was dark and quiet with sleep. With Reed, the silence didn't feel like something that needed to be filled; rather, it felt like something to be shared. Like a secret. Or a kiss.

Reed drew Nor to him. When they pulled apart, he kept his hands on her face. "Ask me what I'm thinking," he murmured.

"What are you thinking?"

He hooked a piece of her wet hair with his finger and tugged on it gently. "That you are so beautiful."

Nor blushed. "Oh, shut up."

"You are so beautiful," Reed continued, ignoring her. "No wonder it hurt to look anywhere else." He kissed her good-bye, pressing his lips to the scars on her wrists.

Nor scooped up Bijou and hurried into the house. Once upstairs, she plopped the little dog onto the bed and threw her sand-filled combat boots into the corner.

Moonlight flooded the room with its opalescent light; from up there, the rest of the island was just shadows, as foreboding as a fairy tale. Monsters may very well have been hiding in those shadows, but with the briny scent of the ocean still on her skin, Nor couldn't imagine how any nightmare could possibly find her that night.

Nor was dreaming again. In her dream, she was standing in a cold and unfamiliar room. The walls and floor were made of stone. The room had a foul odor to it, a mix of rot and decay, and the metallic scent of blood. The only way out was up a winding stone staircase. The only light poured in from a solitary window at the far end of the room.

Nor tapped her red-lacquered nails against her arm. Green fern tattoos spiraled across her pallid skin. Her stilettos clicked menacingly against the cold stone floors as she paced.

Catriona held the victim down and covered the woman's mouth with her hand. A plain girl so used to being overlooked, Catriona had proven to be very useful, devoted, and reliable.

Madge had turned out to be far too fainthearted for such work, Mohawk too stupid. But Catriona, well, she was far too eager for it. She'd probably rip out the woman's tongue with her bare hands if Nor let her.

The woman kneeling on the floor in front of Catriona emitted a pathetic moan, more animal than human. She had the same nose as her son and the same fair hair. And the same too-familiar expression: instead of seeing love in his eyes, there was only ever fear and contempt, a constant reminder that, no matter what she did, time and again what she *wanted* continued to slip through her hands like frayed rope.

"What do you want?" Bliss's voice was a strangled whisper, as if the grip Catriona had on the back of her head affected her ability to speak. Perhaps it did.

"You have nothing I want," Nor snapped in that voice that

did not belong to her, "but you do have something I need." When she was finished with Bliss Sweeney, she would be sure to have carved out any resemblance remaining between mother and son. She would make a point of it.

"Is it the girl?" Bliss asked. "I swear I only spoke to her about the spell once!"

Nor's eyes narrowed. "What do you mean?"

Bliss hesitated. "I — I asked her about casting a spell for me. I haven't seen my son in years. I was desperate. You have to understand, a mother's love is —" She stopped.

"And what was the girl's response?" Nor snapped.

"She insisted she couldn't cast it." Her voice wavered. "Should she be able to?"

"That," Nor said in that honeyed tone, "has yet to be determined." She ran the razor-sharp point of a red fingernail along Bliss Sweeney's soft jawline. "But thank you. You've been more helpful than I expected you to be."

Much later, the blood of Quinn Sweeney's mother trickled across the floor. As promised, there was nothing left of her that resembled her son. There was nothing left of her at all.

Nor wiped the blood from her face. She turned to Catriona, who had a new fern tattoo coiling up her arm like a snake. It was splattered with blood.

"Now," Nor said, "let's talk about the girl."

* * *

The frantic beat of Nor's own heart filled her ears as she pounded down a faint pathway near the southern shore of the island. No one had maintained this trail for years — Nor wasn't entirely sure she'd known it existed before now. The hems of her pajama pants were torn and muddy; there were rips in the long-sleeved T-shirt she'd worn to bed, and chestnut burrs were caught in her hair. Her hands and face were smeared with dirt and blood. The wintry air burned her lungs and turned her breath to mist.

A little fox raced through the woods parallel to her, his thoughts moving in and out of her head. He sped in front of her, and Nor could feel the racing of his heart, the cold air in his lungs. The farther away he got, the harder he was to hear, and all too quickly he was gone, leaving Nor alone in the woods.

Nor yelped as she jammed her bare foot on a rock in the trail. She sank to the ground to assess the damage: a jagged gash on the heel of her right foot. She pressed her hand to the wound, just as she'd watched Judd do a thousand times, but she couldn't get it to mend. Perhaps it was too deep. Perhaps she was too scared.

"What are you doing out here?" a gravelly voice asked. Startled, Nor looked up to see Reuben Finch looming over her.

"I don't know," she answered hoarsely. One minute, she was falling asleep in her own bed. The next, she was waking up in a pile of frost-covered leaves and mud on one of the island's abandoned trails with no memory of how she'd gotten there. And the dream she'd had in between? She was quite certain now that this dream — and the last one — hadn't been dreams at all.

Horror swept over her like a cold sweat. It had been her hand with those red-painted nails that had wiped Bliss Sweeney's blood from her face. She had watched those ferns unfurl from her arm. Only, she didn't have red nails. Or tattoos.

Reuben nodded thoughtfully, as if Nor had given him an answer worth deliberation. His face, Nor noted, was lined with time and endless summers spent outdoors. His eyebrows were as thick and unruly as a briar patch, and his goatee was streaked with the fiery red hair that had once covered his head. "All right then," he said.

He held out his giant hand and pulled Nor to her feet, nearly crushing her fingers with his meaty paw. Her grandparents, Nor realized as she kneaded her smashed hand, were quite similar. Once upon a time, they must have made quite the pair.

Nor stumbled, hopping back and forth on her good foot in an attempt to regain her balance. With Reuben's help, she somehow managed to keep her weight on the ball of her foot, hobble over fallen tree limbs, and pick her way through branches sharp with thorns cloaking the path. When they finally emerged from the woods, Nor was surprised to find they were on the other side of Reuben's farmhouse.

Tucked back from Stars-in-Their-Eyes Lane, the large cabin sat at the very end of the property and was surrounded by acres of farmland. As she limped down the long drive-way, Nor could see fields of bright-green asparagus and red stalks of chard. A few free-range chickens roamed the yard. From here, she could also make out one of the closest neigh-boring isles. Halcyon Island was barely a few miles long and boasted only one structure — the abandoned hotel.

It scared her, all of it: the dream with all that blood on the floor and the fear in Bliss Sweeney's eyes and those red-painted nails scared the shit out of Nor. Those plants, with their bloodthirsty thorns, scared her, too. And there was something disquieting about that uninhabited island.

As soon as Nor walked through the cabin's front door, she smelled oolong tea brewing. She hobbled after Reuben into the kitchen, passing a stone fireplace, a braided rug stretched across the hardwood floors, and a rocking chair in the corner. Aside from the tea, the house smelled of leather and pine and wet wool.

Reuben set a ceramic mug on the table in front of Nor. The mug was large and obviously handmade, misshapen and glazed in a multitude of hues, all turquoise and cerulean and jade. After pulling a first aid kit from one of the kitchen cupboards, Reuben settled into the chair next to Nor. He took her foot in his hand, examining the gash on her heel. "You must have been moving fast," he mused. He wiped the wound clean of dirt, applied a disinfecting salve that made Nor wince, and then wrapped a length of gauze around her foot.

Though Reuben Finch was Nor's biological grandfather, their relationship was a bit untraditional, because neither had ever acknowledged their relationship at all. Traditionally, the fathers of the Blackburn women didn't give so much as a second thought to the daughters they'd sired, let alone their granddaughters. The only difference was that Judd Blackburn, who had loved both men and women at one time or another, and Reuben Finch had been childhood sweethearts. Ironically, the only Blackburn daughter who had ever been conceived in love had been Fern.

"That'll have to do for now," he said. "Let's get you home to Judd so she can fix you up properly."

He pulled her up, and that was when Nor spotted it again — through the window, the little red fox. Satisfied that Nor was safe — at least for now — he darted around the corner of the porch and scurried into the fields and out of sight.

Reuben helped Nor through the back fields toward the Tower. When they reached the gate that divided the woods from Harper Forgette's property, however, he turned and began walking away.

"You're not going to help me the rest of the way?" Nor called.

"Eh, you're strong enough to make it on your own," Reuben answered glibly. And with that, his lumbering stride took him back into the woods.

"Are you kidding me?" Nor muttered. She pulled herself up and over the fence, catching her leg on the barbed wire Harper Forgette used to try to keep raccoons out of the pastures. She landed on the ground with a grunt and stumbled back to her feet. The alpacas weren't quite as pleased to see Nor this time. She was much too distressed for their liking, and the pack turned away with quick, nervous steps. She kept hobbling across the pasture, and the dogs came into view. They were waiting at their usual spot, but Antiquity's attention and hostility, usually aimed at Nor, were directed elsewhere. *That can't possibly be good.*

Suddenly, Pike was hurtling over the gate toward her. "Where in the *hell* have you been?" he asked, gripping her arm.

Nor didn't answer but glanced toward the Tower. An unfamiliar and flashy green car was parked in the front yard.

A familiar panic began to build in her chest. Those scars — those neat little lines that ran along her ankles, in the crook of her arm, along her hips — began to hum in anticipation. "She's here," she said. "Isn't she?"

Pike examined the cuts on Nor's face and noticed the gauze wrapped around her foot. He made a face, grabbed her arm, and wrapped it around his shoulder. The sheathed knife he carried on his hip was thick, like a cleaver or a machete.

"We'll get Judd to heal you up after," he said.

After what?

Protection Spell

"Treat others with respect, and one should seldom be in need
of protection. As for the times when this is not effective,
one should do oneself a favor and get a knife."
— Rona Blackburn

Nor wasn't sure if she was more surprised to find her
mother sitting at one end of the dining room table or to
find Judd sitting across from Fern at the opposite end. It
was an unsettling and incongruous pairing. Judd's mouth
was hardened into her usual scowl. Her calloused hands
were wrapped around a teacup, the grip so tight Nor could
already see cracks beginning to form in the delicate porcelain. Judd still had on her work boots, and a dusting of dried
mud and grime and who knew what else had sloughed off
onto the floor under the table.

Nor cringed when she saw the provocatively fitted suit —
the same sickly green color as the car parked outside — her
mother was wearing. The jacket flared at the hips and

was unbuttoned just enough to expose the edges of a see-through bustier. She had on four-inch heels, the bottoms of which appeared to have been dipped in red. It was the same red as on her nails and lips. Jewels hung from her ears and sparkled on her fingers. Delicate fern tattoos wound around her wrists and fingers. They spiraled over her ears and across the tops of her breasts.

Catriona sat to the right of Fern. She was shockingly thin, skeletal even. Nor could hear the grinding sound of bone on bone when she crossed her legs. Catriona, too, had a fern tattoo, one that coiled up her right arm like a snake. Something red was splattered across that tattoo. Nor swallowed hard. It looked a lot like blood.

The scars on Nor's wrists started to throb. She clung dumbly to Pike as he led her toward the table. He peeled her trembling fingers from his arm, then joined Sena Crowe to stand against the wall.

"Sit down, girlie," Judd said to Nor. Her voice was composed, but judging from the look in her eyes, Nor's grandmother was feeling anything but calm. The dogs seemed to agree; Antiquity was hiding under the table, her hackles up, her ears back. Bijou was glued to a spot by the front door.

"Nor," Fern purred. "I'm so glad you could join us."

She held out a hand so unnaturally white it was as if embalming fluid coursed through her veins. Nor wasn't sure what she was supposed to do. Kiss her hand? Bow? Instead, she mutely sank into the chair next to Apothia. Nor's scars were screaming so loudly, she could barely hear anything else.

"Just breathe," Apothia muttered, leaning toward Nor. "Everything is going to be fine."

Of course we'll be fine, Nor thought, momentarily reassured. *We have the Giantess.*

"All right, Fern," Judd said. "Cut to the chase. What're ya doing here?"

Nor breathed a sigh of relief as soon as she heard the fierceness in her grandmother's tone. All Nor had to do was hide in the safety of Judd's shadow, and the Giantess would take care of everything else.

Fern feigned hurt and surprise. "Why, you are my *family*." She opened her arms wide in an exaggerated gesture of amiability. She turned to Nor and, in a voice dripping with honey, said, "I'm here to visit my lovely daughter, of course."

It was the way she said *my lovely daughter* that made the hair on the back of Nor's neck prickle. Fern stood, and her tattoos began to writhe. They slithered from her skin and skulked across the table toward Nor, and Nor eyed them nervously, feeling like a flower about to be plucked, an animal about to be butchered.

"So, tell me, Nor," Fern said, "what Burden did our great matriarch bestow on my offspring?" She laughed at Nor's answer with a shrill cackle. "I suppose we heard right," she said to Catriona. "She really isn't any threat, is she?" A vine lashed out suddenly and latched onto Nor's arm. Like a stretching cat, it unfurled its spiny fronds and clawed at her sleeves.

Judd stood abruptly, which sent her chair skidding across the floor. At her full formidable height, Judd towered over her daughter by at least a foot, even with Fern's four-inch stilettos. "Fern!" she commanded, her booming voice echoing off the vaulted ceiling. "You let her go!"

"Mother, please," Fern said with a yawn, "we're just having a little fun. Besides, we both know you can't control me any more now than when I was younger." To prove her point, she gave a flick of her tongue, which had the effect of slamming Judd to the ground and trapping her there. The Tower rattled with the force of her fall. Antiquity skidded out from under the table and stood over Judd protectively. The dog bared her teeth and growled, a low rumble that shook the windows like thunder.

"It *is* a shame," Fern said, turning to Nor, who was struggling against the fern. "It's almost as if no magic courses through your veins."

The thorns of the vine burrowed into Nor's arm. The pain was white-hot and impossible. Fern was just playing with her now, causing pain simply because she enjoyed it, simply to remind Nor that she could.

Nor screamed, and Pike and Sena Crowe leaped into action. Sena Crowe hacked at the stalk with his knife until just a part of the hilt remained in his hand. The rest of the curved blade was now stuck fast in the thick, unyielding stem. Pike grabbed the vine with both hands and tried pulling it away from Nor's skin.

Fern sighed and leaned into Nor. "You know they'll only succeed if I decide to let them," she said. Her breath was sickly sweet, like overripe fruit. "I won't, but it *is* fun to watch them try."

Fern laughed as Sena Crowe began to wheeze, and Pike's grasp on the fern weakened. Apothia's eyes rolled back in her head, and she slumped over. Fern's power was thick like sludge. Nor waited for the nausea to hit her, that blurred sense of intoxication, the loss of focus, the difficulty breathing. But it never came. Nor could feel her magic pushing against Fern's. And for the first time, instead of giving in to her fear — the kind of fear that used to make Nor want to slide a sharp object across her skin — she gave in to her own power.

Nor's magic coursed, unharnessed, through her veins. It was a raging fire, a wild animal, an impenetrable shield. Fern's control slid off her like dirty dishwater.

Nor's eyes fell on Sena Crowe's knife, still lodged in the vine. Nor tugged it free, then started swinging. She hacked at the thick stalk wrapped around her arm until it finally stiffened and dropped to the table, a withered husk. Fern had stopped laughing.

Pike and Sena Crow recovered their breath and gasped. Apothia opened her eyes and coughed. Judd, no longer under Fern's control, rushed to her side, but Apothia waved her off, then poured herself a cup of tea with trembling hands. Catriona gaped at the shriveled fern.

Fern stretched her arms over her head in an attempt at nonchalance, but her anger was palpable, a bloated behemoth that she couldn't hide from Nor. It was in the clench of her jaw, the pulsing vein in her forehead, the bloodied half-moons she'd gouged into her own arms.

She stared at Nor and the dead vine, then silently stormed out of the Tower. Catriona stumbled in her haste to follow.

As soon as the door closed, Nor sank back into her chair. Her hands were shaking.

Judd pointed at Sena Crowe and Pike, both battered and bloodied. "Go," she said, coughing. "Make sure she isn't coming back."

Sena Crowe and Pike both nodded and quickly disappeared through the front door.

Judd sat down next to Nor and examined her injuries. She ran her calloused palm against the abrasions on Nor's collarbone and the scratches on the side of her face. The wounds started to heal, and so much steam was in the air that Nor could barely see Judd's face.

Judd then pulled Nor's foot into her lap and probed the deep gash. Nor winced. A viscous substance overflowed Judd's palms and spilled onto the floor.

"Now," she said, wiping her hands on her jeans, "lemme

see about that last bit." Nor's arms looked as if they'd been wrapped in barbed wire. When Judd pulled her hands away, long quills came with them.

"That was a mighty stupid thing to do, girlie," Judd said to Nor when she was finished. "If Fern was, as she said, here to see *you*, then you certainly gave her something worth seeing. In fact, I can bet that you've piqued her interest now."

"What do you mean?" Nor examined her foot. No blood, no cut, no scar.

"You ruined her fun," Judd said. "And you fought back. You fought her off." She eyed Nor with interest. "Not many can do that."

"It's possible that she regards you as a threat now, dear," Apothia added.

"A threat?" Nor balked. "I'm not a threat!"

"I wouldn't go so far as to say that," Judd replied. Nor shifted uncomfortably under her grandmother's gaze.

"Is there something you want to tell me?" Judd asked.

Nor quickly shook her head.

"So we're just chalking it up to dumb luck, then? Fine." Judd grunted. "If that's the case, as soon as Pike and Sena Crowe return, I'm having them haul your ass up to the Coldwater place before that luck runs out."

"If Fern returns —" Nor started.

"If Fern returns, then I guess we'll just have to hope that dumb luck of yours rubs off on the rest of us."

"Why don't you go pack up a few things?" Apothia said, gently pushing Nor toward the stairs. "Maybe take a shower while you're at it."

Nor reached up to touch the gash on Apothia's cheek. How much worse might it have gotten had Nor not reached for that blade?

"You should ask Judd to heal this for you," she said, but when she took her hand away, the wound was gone, and her own fingers were covered in glossy strands like spun sugar. Apothia raised her hand to her healed cheek, but didn't say a word.

Bijou followed Nor into the bathroom. Nor shut and locked the door, and Bijou curled up against the heating vent in the wall. Years ago, Astrid, the fifth daughter, had paneled these walls with cedar, but the room had long ago lost that clean and woodsy scent. Now it had a musty odor that clung to the towels and to Bijou's fur when he spent too much time sleeping against the vent.

Nor peeled off her torn clothes, tossed them into a corner, and stepped into the shower. She washed her hair twice, combing out the burrs with her fingers. She sank to the bottom. The scalding water poured over her and rinsed all the blood and grime down the drain.

She got out and wiped the fog from the mirror. Her skin was red and blotchy from the hot water. Her hair dripped down her back.

"What did you do?" she muttered at her reflection. She could feel her magic still pulsing under her skin like a heart-beat. Her hands shook with the power of it. What would happen if her mother returned? Could she fight her off again? Nor wasn't sure. Was she strong enough to carry all these Burdens on her own?

Or would they swallow her whole?

In her bedroom, Nor stuffed some clothes into a duffel bag. After hearing someone on the staircase — probably Pike or maybe Sena Crowe — she quickly slipped on a pair of jeans and put an old army jacket on over her damp skin. She grabbed her phone — dead, of course — and her necklace with the crow's claw off the top of the dresser, scooped up Bijou, and clomped down the stairs in her combat boots.

Sena Crowe was waiting for her in the stairwell at the second floor. Without a word, he reached out and took the duffel bag from her shoulders. "You good?" he asked. She nodded. They both knew she was lying.

Judd was sitting in a chair by the window, smoking her pipe. Nor needed her grandmother to be formidable and fearsome. She needed the Giantess, not this worn-down woman staring out the window.

"Here," Nor said awkwardly to Apothia, trying to hand Bijou off to her. "He throws a fit when I leave him behind."

Apothia kissed her cheeks and pushed Bijou back into Nor's arms. "Then you should take him with you."

Nor nodded. She glanced at Judd one last time and then

followed Sena Crowe. Outside, the naked trees shuddered in the wind.

Pike turned the key and — after a few false starts — the engine of the yellow Jeep sputtered to life. It gave a lurch, and soon the three of them were bumping down Meandering Lane. The cold seeped in through the Jeep's open doorframe, and Nor pulled her jacket tighter. The Sweet and Savory Bakery was empty. Outside the Willowbark General Store, a discarded umbrella swung forlornly from the porch railing. It seemed only the Witching Hour was still open, though there didn't appear to be any customers inside. Or anywhere for that matter.

They came to a stop before turning onto Red Poppy Road. Nor couldn't hear any birds chirping or leaves rustling. Bijou whined softly; he didn't like the unnatural quiet. Neither did Nor. It felt as if the entire island was holding its breath. As if, like Nor, it too was trying to determine if the danger had passed.

They continued driving in silence. At one point, Pike suddenly veered, taking the Jeep off road. Nor clung to the sides of her seat as they bounced over the rough terrain. Branches whipped at her face and arms. And just as Nor was beginning to think the island was far larger — and wilder — than she'd ever known, the trees finally gave way to a large circular clearing.

Pike parked along the perimeter. He grabbed Nor's

duffel bag, swung it easily onto his shoulder, and motioned for her to follow him and Sena Crowe toward the largest of the fifteen or so houses scattered throughout the area.

Most of the houses, while well kept, looked as though they were originally built a century ago, with lacy peaked roofs and pointed windows and doors like those of a cathedral. Equal parts sparse and elaborate, the houses brought to mind a gingerbread house. The kind of house a fairy-tale witch might live in.

The thought struck Nor as extremely funny. She started to laugh, but then composed herself before Pike and Sena Crowe could decide she'd gone completely crazy.

They passed by a grandiose fountain in the shape of a woman holding a giant bowl above her head. It was more than double the height of even the tallest of the houses. Water spilled from the bowl onto the woman's breasts and into the basin at her feet. She wasn't the only statue on the compound. Each house also had its own wooden sculpture. Most were beasts — a mix of real and imaginary: a bison with the wings of a bat, a brown bear with ox horns, a wild cat with the barbed tail of a dragon and the forked tongue of a snake, a horse with the head of an eagle.

The creepiest was what looked like a woman with abnormally long legs and arms that hung all the way to the ground. Her clawed fingers were curled as if awaiting something to grip or to strangle. This one was faceless, its features charred as if they'd been burned off.

"They're supposed to be frightening," a voice called.

Charlie was making her way toward Nor from across the compound. To Nor's dismay, Gage followed closely behind, a scowl on his face.

"At least, that was the intention," Charlie said, coming up beside her. She patted the leg of the statue fondly. "Rona called them our aegises."

"Aegises," Nor mused. "That's from Greek mythology, isn't it?" She was ignoring Gage's dark look, the one burning a hole in the side of her face. Even if her hair caught fire, she would not turn her head. *It's not my fault I'm here,* she wanted to say. *It's not like I was given a choice.* "The aegis was the name of the shield that protected Athena," Nor said instead. "She was the goddess of wisdom and of warfare."

Charlie nodded. "And just like the aegis was made to protect Athena, Rona made our aegises to protect us."

"She made them to protect *herself,*" Gage grumbled. He gestured with his cigarette. "That we also benefit from their protection was just an accidental but fortunate by-product." Angrily, he stabbed out his cigarette on the statue's leg. Almost as an afterthought, he brushed off the ash before storming away.

"I always feel better about my place in the world after talking to him," Nor said.

"It'd probably be best to ignore him today," Charlie said. "He's pissed off that Dauphine still won't let me or him join Pike and Sena Crowe on their patrols."

"Patrols of what?"

"Well, you've noticed the change on the island, right? The plants and the weather and the whales disappearing? Whatever's causing it — whether it's your mother or something else — we're betting isn't anything benevolent or benign. For weeks now we've been sweeping the island to make sure we aren't caught unaware. Did a whole lot of good, though."

"Why's that?"

"Your mom got on the island anyway, didn't she?" Charlie pointed out. "But I guess that's kind of her whole deal, huh? Getting people to do what she wants? She didn't want us to know she was coming, so we didn't." She caught Nor's arm before they went inside. "But hey, don't worry. We were made for this. We keep the Blackburn women safe, even if it's from another Blackburn woman. It's our duty. Our —"

"Burden," Nor finished for her.

Charlie shrugged. "Depends on how you look at it, I guess. Do me a favor, though, and try not to take Gage too seriously. He does enough of that all by himself. But like the rest of us, there is a part of him that's glad you're safe. Granted, it is a very small part," she admitted, "but I believe it exists."

Nor looked up at the monstrous figure looming over them. From this angle, the statue seemed to block the entire sky. "Sure it does," she replied softly.

* * *

All too soon, Nor found herself cloistered in the finished basement of Dauphine Coldwater's house. From the few windows that sat high along the basement's walls, Nor watched night fall; every half hour or so a pair of feet passed along with the sweep of a flashlight.

Pike and Sena Crowe sat on the stairs, spitting sunflower shells into an empty Coke bottle. Dauphine's wolfhound — whom they ridiculously referred to as *Steve* — was stretched out at the bottom of the stairs. To the common observer, the great beast appeared to be sleeping, but his ears were pricked, as if all his energy were being expended on listening.

The basement was crowded with old boxes and mismatched furniture. Worn couches were draped in colorful tapestries. There was a pool table, a rip in the center of its green felted top. A broken-down piano sat in a corner. A casbah lantern cast elaborate diamonds across the walls.

Gage flopped onto one of the ancient couches, and Charlie settled herself on one of the pillows littering the floor. She pulled out a deck of tarot cards from her pocket. The cards were soft with wear. With expert hands, she quickly shuffled the deck and then drew out three cards and set them in a row on the ground in front of her. "The first card represents what's happening now," she explained to Nor, flipping it over. "The Five of Swords typically points to conflict, tension, and betrayal. Sound about right so far?"

Nor nodded skeptically. Gage let out an exasperated sigh.

Charlie ignored him. "This one will tell us what we need to do about it." She flipped over the second card and furrowed her brow. "Hmm, the Hanged Man is the willing victim. It typically represents self-sacrifice, but," she was quick to add, "that shouldn't be taken literally."

She moved to the third card. "And this should tell us the outcome." Charlie flipped over the card, revealing a picture of a burning tower. The color drained from her face. She plucked the cards off the floor and stuffed the deck back into her pocket.

"What is it?" Nor asked. "What's wrong?"

"Nothing." Charlie's face had turned from white to pink. "It's just a silly hobby. I obviously have no talent for tarot whatsoever."

Something told Nor she did, but she didn't push it. Whatever that card meant, Nor could bet it wasn't anything good.

"But I promise you don't have anything to worry about," Charlie said to Nor, smiling. "You're safer here than anywhere else."

"Anywhere else on the island, you mean?" Nor asked.

Charlie waved her hand in the air. "I mean, anywhere else *anywhere.*"

"It's charmed," Gage explained. "Undetectable. Another gift from the benevolent Rona Blackburn." The sarcasm in his voice was so thick, Charlie hit him with a pillow.

"If someone were to seek us out without having been invited," Charlie continued, "they'd just drive around and around the lake until they mysteriously found themselves back on the main part of the island."

"So even if Fern wanted to find me —"

"She wouldn't be able to."

"I gotta say," Pike said from the stairs, "you gave her a good fight. Don't you think, Sena Crowe?"

Nor thought of her magic guiltily. Though it seemed to be subdued for now, she could still feel it vibrating underneath her skin. Like the wolfhound, it too was on alert. Why Nor was able to resist her mother's coercion was something she didn't want to talk about or have examined too closely. Nor searched for a topic of distraction. She pointed at the wolfhound lying at the bottom of the stairs. "You do know that Steve's not his name, right?"

Pike patted the dog's large head. "Of course it is. We gave it to him."

"What is it then?" Charlie asked anyway.

"Burn," Nor said simply.

"Burn?" Pike repeated.

"Yes, Burn. He's over a hundred years old, and you all seriously thought his name was *Steve?*"

The room was silent for a moment, then erupted in laughter.

"Burn. No shit," Pike exclaimed. "Well, that is a lot

better than Steve, isn't it, boy? To Burn!" he toasted, holding the Coke bottle full of sunflower shells in the air.

"To Burn!" they all exclaimed.

"So what's he thinking now?" Pike asked Nor excitedly.

"That you're an asshole," Sena Crowe answered. "You don't need to be able to read his mind to know that."

While everyone else in the room laughed again, Nor climbed into a musty-smelling sleeping bag and snuck a peek at her phone. She'd forgotten to plug it in. *Of course.* There was no easy way of getting in touch with Savvy. Or with Reed.

It wasn't much later when the lights in the room went out. Charlie and Gage had both returned to their own houses to sleep in their own beds. Gage had left without saying a word.

Nor listened to the crunching of footsteps on the gravel outside the basement window and to the low murmurs of Pike and Sena Crowe talking quietly at the top of the stairs. Bijou curled up on Nor's pillow. Nor rolled over onto her back and stared at the ceiling. Though she may have been safer here, she wanted to be in her own room. She wanted to be able to see the moon. All she could see here was a water stain that looked to Nor like a knife. She fiddled with the crow's claw, slid it back and forth along its chain, and tried to remember a time when she'd felt more alone.

12

Spell for Courage

"Courage, once found, should always be encouraged to stay."
—Rona Blackburn

What are you doing?" Gage asked, his voice thick with ennui. The two of them stood facing each other at opposite ends of a training mat set up in a secluded spot at the edge of the compound. They'd been at it for hours. Sweat dripped down Nor's back. The sun was setting low over the horizon, and Nor envied its chance at a reprieve. Gage's arms were crossed. "I keep telling you. You have to plant your feet."

Nor looked down. "I did," she insisted.

"No, you didn't. If your feet were planted, your attacker wouldn't be able to do *this*." And with that, he stepped forward, grabbed her wrist, spun her around, and stepped on the back of her knee. She yelped and dropped to the ground with a thud. By the time Nor had gotten her bearings, Gage already had a fistful of her hair clutched in one hand and a knife against her throat.

Asking Gage to spend any time with her was asking for more grief than Nor needed. But this morning when he had said he doubted Nor could defend herself against a Jack Russell terrier — to use his words — Nor had insisted on proving him wrong.

It was a decision she regretted now more than anything.

It had been almost three weeks since Nor had moved onto the compound. She was allowed to leave only if she had an escort — namely Pike or the taciturn Sena Crowe — with her. She'd barely seen Judd or Apothia and barely spoken to Savvy. Reed thought she was spending time with family. Nor hated lying to him, but what was she supposed to say? *Oh, you know, just your typical family drama — I'm pretty sure my mom wants to kill me, so I'm just hiding out for a bit.* At least when she talked to Savvy she could tell the truth.

Nor pulled herself up and assessed herself for injuries. She had fresh bruises on her knees, but most of the damage had been to her ego.

Gage sighed. "You're fine. That's what the mat's for." He spun his knife on the tip of his finger by its point.

Nor cursed him silently. "I didn't know you had a knife."

"Oh, I'm sorry," he scoffed. "I'm sure whoever you're defending yourself against will be sure to tell you exactly what weapons they're carrying. But okay. Let's try a different tactic. You take the knife." He flipped the blade easily in his hand and handed it to her, hilt first.

Nor gawped at it. "I — I don't want it," she insisted. Her fingertips itched to grasp the hilt, to touch the coolness of the blade. Apothia had been right to keep the knives hidden.

"Just take it."

"No," she said, backing up. She stared at the gleaming knife, her heart pounding too fast and too hard in her chest.

"Jesus, Nor. Take the damn knife!"

She grabbed the knife from him and immediately threw it to the ground. "I don't want it!" Tears welled up in her eyes. She swiped at them angrily. "Fine! You win, all right?" she screamed at Gage. "I'm no good at this!"

Gage spat and snatched the weapon from the ground. He stabbed the knife into the leg of one of the statues, then stalked off. Blood welled up from the slice Nor had cut into her palm.

Later that night, Nor lay on the couch in Dauphine's basement. The occasional murmur of voices from upstairs drifted over her. The old house creaked and moaned. Bijou, curled up on her pillow, shifted in his sleep. The tiniest tip of tongue stuck out from between his teeth.

Nor scrolled through her phone mindlessly before tossing it to the side with a sigh. No one had seen Fern anywhere even close to the archipelago, not since her visit to the Tower to see Nor. In fact, no one had seen her anywhere lately. The sales of *The Price Guide to the Occult* had skyrocketed, her seminars were sold out all over the country, and yet the woman herself hadn't been seen in weeks. Then there was that event in Chicago: people were alarmed at Fern Blackburn's inability to cast one of her own spells. Instead of being relieved at this turn, Nor felt more frightened than before; while their encounter at the Tower had clearly weakened her mother, Nor could feel her magic raging like a wildfire under her skin.

She gently prodded the bruises on her face and fiddled with the gauze wrapped around her hand. She hadn't been able to heal her own injuries, as minor as they were. Part of her wondered if that was because she didn't want them to heal. She thought about the cold steel blade of Gage's knife. For Nor, cutting had been a habit, a routine solution she'd reached for every time she felt afraid. No matter how many times she'd tried to let it go, it still somehow remained, a final resort she struggled to resist. *How can I expect to defend myself against other people*, she wondered, *when I'm so busy trying to protect myself — from myself?*

When Nor finally fell asleep, she dreamed she was back at the Tower. Reed was waiting for her downstairs, but the only thing hanging in her closet was that black bustier dress. She put it on and found not Reed, but Gage waiting in the kitchen with Savvy.

Before Nor could ask why they were there, she looked

down to see blood covering her arms. She tried to wipe it away and find the source, but it was thick as paint.

"I told you you'd never find love if you're always covered in blood," Savvy said.

Nor screamed for help, and the other two watched indifferently as Nor's blood continued to drip from her arms onto the floor and spread.

The dream changed.

Nor was now standing in the Witching Hour. The shop was empty and dark. The waning light of the moon spilled through a window streaked with dirt and grime and what looked like bird shit.

She swept her arm along one shelf after another and sent candles, crystals, and row after row of tiny deities — Baphomet and Hecate, the Mother Goddess and Cernunnos, the horned one — crashing to the ground. She waded through the broken glass and porcelain, grinding tiny divine arms and legs into dust with the sharp points of her stiletto heels.

There was movement from the back of the shop, and a putrid stench filled the air. Nor turned and instantly regretted it.

Once upon a time, Madge had been a truly beautiful woman. Her skin now sagged like melted candle wax. Her face resembled a jack-o'-lantern left to rot in the rain. A lattice of black scabs crisscrossed her arms and legs. Her tattoos oozed with infection.

"I told you," the creature with Madge's voice said. "I don't know where she is. I haven't seen her in weeks."

"How can I be sure that you aren't lying to me?"

"I wouldn't!" Madge gasped. "Not to you. Not about this." Madge glanced at Nor's arm. Where once there had been a tattoo was only a gruesome wound in the shape of a fern.

The memory of a dried-up fern lying on Judd's table flashed across Nor's mind. And then something else: a convention hall in Chicago packed with thousands of people, millions more watching on a live stream. She'd plucked an eager young man from the audience. The spell he'd requested had been a simple transmutation spell: relatively easy to cast, but still impressive.

The spell hadn't worked. The man had remained unaltered. He was quickly escorted from the stage while she stormed offstage, awash in fury and humiliation. She could hear doubt rising from the audience. She could see it in the eyes of those waiting for her backstage.

There hadn't been any reason for the spell to fail. The power of Bliss Sweeney's sacrifice should have still coursed through her veins, but even the wounds she'd later carved into Catriona's arms had done nothing but bolster her anger. She couldn't cast the Revulsion Curse, the Wish-Granting Charm, or even Void of Reason, a spell aided by opium seeds. The only way she could conjure the Mouthful of Ashes jinx was to throw the ashes into the person's mouth herself. Most alarmingly, even the spell she'd cast over Quinn was becoming more difficult to maintain. It was all she could do to keep that spell fed.

With enough spilled blood, there shouldn't have been any spell she couldn't cast, no rapacious desire she couldn't fulfill. Something had happened. Something that had started with the girl and that vanquished fern. Blood could ooze from the walls or bubble up from the floor, and she suspected there would be no effect. And it filled Nor with cold desperation.

"You've always been quite fond of the girl, haven't you?" Nor asked in her mother's voice. "And even as a little girl, she was fond of you."

"Th-that's true," Madge stammered.

"And yet she hasn't told you where she's hiding." Nor clucked her tongue. "Be honest with me. You don't want me to know, do you?"

Madge blinked at her nervously. "What do you mean?"

"You were hoping that maybe I would just let her go? That I would move on. Didn't you?"

Madge lowered her head in shame. "I will find her for you," she promised between sobs.

"I'm afraid that's no longer an option." Tattoos unfurled from Nor's skin. They attacked like cobras. Thorns, venomous and sharp as teeth, struck at Madge's throat.

Nor left the Witching Hour alone, branding the staircase with bloody footprints.

Nor woke with a start, her pulse racing. In her mind's eye, she could still see the bloody footprints she'd made on the stairs of the Witching Hour.

Nor swallowed hard. She reached for her phone and dialed Madge. She got her voice mail.

Daylight poured into the room through the basement windows. She could hear car doors slamming outside, the crunch of tires against gravel, and the sound of Pike and Gage arguing.

"You heard what Dauphine said, cuz," Pike was saying.

"Dauphine's being unreasonable," Gage shot back.

Nor ascended the stairs. Standing with Pike and Gage were Sena Crowe and Charlie. "What's going on?" she asked Charlie quietly.

"My brothers are going off island for a bit," Charlie explained.

"And Gage wants to go, but they won't let him?"

"Right. He's taking the news well, don't you think?" Charlie said.

"You make a good point," Pike said to Gage. "If you and Charlie really want to come with us —"

"Really?" Charlie exclaimed.

Pike laughed. "Hell no!" He looked at Sena Crowe. "Can you imagine explaining that one to Dauphine?"

"She'd have our hides, man," Sena Crowe said evenly.

"Exactly. Sorry, cuz. It's out of the question."

Gage pushed past everyone and stomped down the stairs into the basement. Pike was still laughing as he and Sena Crowe left.

Charlie and Nor followed Gage into the basement. Gage plopped onto the couch. He pulled Nor's pillow out from under him and tossed it forcefully onto the floor.

"Where are they going?" Nor dared to ask.

"Dauphine wants them to do a sweep of the entire archipelago," Charlie answered. "I wouldn't worry about it, though. It's fairly routine."

"Do you think Pike and Sena Crowe will be gone long enough to give us time to get to the other side of the island and back?" Nor asked.

Gage raised an eyebrow.

Nor took a deep breath. "I want to go to the Witching Hour."

"Fresh out of eye of newt, are you?" Gage said with a sneer.

Nor gave him a look. "I can't get ahold of Madge. I want to check in on her."

"I'm going to need more of a reason than that," he said.

"I just have a bad feeling," Nor insisted. "That's reason enough. If you don't want to come with me, I'll go by myself."

"Like hell you will," Gage snapped.

"Hang on," Charlie said. "Do you realize how pissed off Pike will be if you leave the compound?"

"And you listen to him about as much as —" Nor paused to let Gage and Charlie think it over.

"I can't think of a time when we've ever listened to him, can you?" Gage asked Charlie.

"Doesn't ring any bells," Charlie admitted.

"So you're in?" Nor asked.

Charlie grinned. "Yeah, we're in."

"Any idea how we're getting there?" Gage asked Nor.

Nor hadn't thought of that. "I'll text Savvy about finding us a ride," she decided quickly.

"Does she have a boat?" Charlie asked.

"She has a Vespa, but Savvy's resourceful. She'll figure out something."

A few moments later, Nor, Gage, and Charlie left the basement and made their way toward the trees at the edge of the compound. Only the vacant eyes of Rona's aegises witnessed their departure.

When the three emerged on the other side of the trees, they found an old white pickup truck waiting for them. The truck had a long crack in the windshield and, as with most vehicles on the island, was covered with rust. Grayson and Savvy sat in the front seat. Standing outside and leaning against the passenger door was Reed.

Nor smiled in spite of herself. She'd known she could count on Savvy.

Reed unhitched himself from the truck, smiling that crooked grin of his. Nor wrapped her arms tightly around his neck and buried her face in his shoulder.

"Hi," he said, his voice a susurrus in her hair. "These must be your — cousins?" he asked when they pulled apart. He nodded toward Gage and Charlie. Gage snorted.

Nor shot Gage a look. "Something like that," Nor said.

Savvy jumped out of the truck, her electric-blue box braids swinging past her waist. Her face softened when she saw the welts on Nor's face. "Oh. Now *you* look like a villain in a comic book. Which," she added quickly, "you can totally pull off."

"Nice to see you, too," Nor said, smiling.

Reed stroked Nor's bruised cheek.

Nor smiled. "I'm okay," she insisted.

Grayson grinned at them from the driver's seat. "Shut up," Reed mumbled to him, but he didn't take his eyes off Nor.

Grayson laughed. "What?" He swept fast-food wrappings from the seat onto the floor to make room for Nor. "I didn't say anything."

Savvy settled herself atop an ice cooler in the bed of the truck, looking like a dairy princess on a parade float. Charlie and Gage climbed over the side to join her.

"I take it you know where we're headed," Gage said, his tone even more steely than usual. He was staring at Reed's hand, which was resting on Nor's knee.

"The Witching Hour, right?" Reed asked Nor.

"Yeah," she answered, her heart pounding.

Grayson pulled the truck onto the dirt road. Through the passenger window, Nor spotted a little red fox quickening its pace to keep up with them. Nor wondered if it was right in thinking that going in search of Madge was a horrible mistake.

Resurrection Spell

"One should concentrate on living such that when death arrives, one can depart with no apprehension and no regrets."
— Rona Blackburn

Grayson pulled the truck onto Meandering Lane and slowly drove through the fog that had fallen on that side of the island. It was so opaque, Nor could swirl it into shapes with her fingertips. What shapes would they be? An eye for caution, a hand outstretched in warning, a question mark for *What the hell are you doing?*

"The whole street lost power about a week ago," Reed said. "That's when even Mom's regular clients stopped coming. She decided to close up for a bit and visit my aunt Luiza in Florida. She wanted me and Grayson to go with her." He shrugged. "The way things have been around here, Grayson probably should have."

They stopped in front of the Sweet and Savory Bakery. The front door was slightly ajar. A carpet of dried leaves and pinecones covered the bakery floor.

Gage and Charlie jumped out of the back of the truck. "You three should wait for us here," Gage said, pointing at Savvy, Grayson, and Reed.

Savvy opened her mouth to protest, but Nor quickly cut her off. "He's right," she said lightly. "You should just stay put. We won't be long." *Hopefully.*

"But I have this," Reed said, holding up a high-beam flashlight he'd dug out of the debris on the truck floor. "I imagine the Witching Hour can be pretty creepy in the dark." He was teasing her, but when he saw the look on her face, he changed his tone. "Okay," he said somberly, handing her the flashlight. "I'll have Grayson park the truck in front of Willowbark. We'll be there if you need us."

Nor nodded. She glanced over at the stairs and saw a red smear on the handrail. She suspected that when all this was over, none of them would be able to stop associating her with pain. Including herself.

The plants in the front garden bristled as Charlie, Nor, and Gage walked by. The blossoms of a quince bush snapped and hissed. A hawthorn tree, its naked limbs covered in treacherous-looking thorns, loomed menacingly over the staircase. The once-purple blooms of a French lavender bush looked like the husks of dead bees.

"You said you had a bad feeling?" Gage said. "How bad?"

"Pretty bad," Nor whispered.

Gage nodded thoughtfully. "Got it."

Charlie unzipped her sweatshirt and took out a rolled leather bundle she had secured to her chest. Nor watched in awe as Charlie unfurled the bundle, revealing six gleaming knives of various shapes and sizes.

"Do you always carry an arsenal with you?" Nor asked.

Charlie adjusted a serrated blade tucked in her boot. "It's a precaution."

They climbed the stairs. Though the rain had washed some of them away, bloody footprints led down the steps. Nor's heart beat wildly as Gage opened the door.

The dark purple walls seemed to absorb all the light from the flashlight. The air was dank, heavy with a familiar metallic odor. The velvet curtains had been torn to shreds. The floor crunched beneath their feet. Death masks and gargoyles hanging on the wall grinned down at them menacingly.

Something brushed up against Nor's leg. She jumped and let out a stifled yelp.

"Oh shit," she breathed. "It's just Kikimora." She put her hand on Gage's arm to keep him from stabbing the cat.

Nor leaned down and stroked Kikimora's fur. Her hand came away wet, sticky, and warm. Blood. And it wasn't Kiki's. The cat darted out the open door.

Nor scanned the room with her flashlight. Chaos, splattered blood, then finally —

Madge. Slumped on the floor behind the front counter.

"Nor —" Gage said.

Nor didn't hear the rest of what he might have said. She stumbled across the room. *Please don't be dead,* she thought. *Please don't be dead.*

Madge's face was bloated. Her skin was covered entirely with fern tattoos. Blood seeped from lacerations on her arms and legs and puncture wounds on her neck.

Madge emitted a gurgled cough, and Nor set the flashlight to the side and pulled the debased woman's head onto her lap. Nor gasped at the waves of pain she picked up just from touching Madge's fevered skin. Nor stroked her hair, and Madge's agony filled the space between them like scalding steam.

But when Nor pulled her hand away, strands of Madge's once-lustrous hair came with it. Nor swallowed a wave of nausea, wiped her hand clean, and resolutely pushed it against the wounds on Madge's throat. Nor drew out Madge's pain as two long quills. Madge's wounds closed, and she took in a slow, ragged breath.

Nor sighed in relief. She ignored the shocked looks on Charlie's and Gage's faces, and quickly pulled the quills out of her hands. Each one left behind a deep, bloodied gouge. She'd hardly alleviated any of Madge's pain, but she wasn't sure if she could do much more. Pain couldn't heal pain — at least that was what Judd had always said.

"Nor?" Madge rasped. She peered up at Nor, her eyes

mad with fever. "Oh, Nor, I thought she was going to kill me," she said, sobbing.

"You're going to be okay," Nor promised. She looked over at Gage and Charlie. "We need to get her to my grandmother," she said. "And then —"

Madge suddenly sat up and pitched herself at Nor. Nor's palms collided with the floor. Broken glass cut into her hands. Madge wedged a sharp knee into her side, and Nor screamed.

The rest came as a blur. Charlie charged at Madge and sent her flying off Nor with a teeth-rattling blow. Madge hit the counter with a grunt and knocked the cash register to the floor. It did nothing to slow her down. Charlie tackled Madge again, and Gage grabbed Nor from behind and pulled her out of the way.

"Get back!" Gage barked.

Nor scurried to hide behind a bookcase while Gage went to help Charlie. Someone kicked over the flashlight, and the room went dark. The sounds of a struggle continued.

Nor crawled out from behind the bookcase, sliding her hand across the floor in search of the flashlight. She found it, and the light quaked in her trembling hand. She turned it on and aimed it at the noise.

Madge had her hands around Gage's throat. His face was red. His eyes were bulging. A strangled cry escaped his lips. Beside them, Charlie pulled herself to her knees, then slipped and fell. Blood covered the floor.

It was all so familiar: blood and pain and fear.

Nor felt something building inside her, something dark and terrible. It scratched and bit and pulled at her insides. It was so powerful Nor was afraid it would eat her alive if she didn't let it out. She opened her mouth and —

For a moment, it was as if all the sound had been sucked from the room. And then Nor's scream crashed down on everyone like a wave. The floor undulated. The whole building shuddered. The death masks and gargoyles fell from the walls. A window shattered.

And then it was over.

On wobbly legs, Nor staggered across the room toward the other three, grateful to see that Madge, now unconscious, no longer had her hands around Gage's throat. She pulled Gage and Charlie to their feet. "We gotta get out of here," she said. She wasn't sure if either of them could hear her. Charlie had a dazed look on her face. There was a little blood trickling from one of Gage's ears. Nor put her hands on either side of his head. His pain erupted into blisters across her already bleeding palms.

Gage gave her a stunned look. "How did you —" he started.

Nor pushed him toward the door. "Just go!" she said.

It was only after they'd left that Nor allowed herself to look back at Madge sprawled across the floor. She wasn't moving. Nor couldn't tell if she was breathing, but her eyes were closed. Her face looked almost peaceful. Almost.

Nor knew it was likely she'd never see her alive again.

Nor turned and raced after Charlie and Gage. The glass from the Witching Hour's broken window crunched under their feet as they ran down Meandering Lane. They leaped into the back of the truck, landing beside a gaping Savvy.

"Did you hear that noise?" Savvy asked. "What the hell was that? Wait, Nor, what's wrong with your hands —"

"Just drive," Gage ordered.

Grayson started the engine. The truck launched down Stars-in-Their-Eyes Lane, and Charlie breathed a shaky sigh of relief as Meandering Lane quickly faded into the distance.

Gage leaned over to examine Nor's hands. "Here, let me see." For the first time, when he looked at her, Nor didn't see resentment in his face but genuine concern. Or maybe it was awe. Either way, it made her uncomfortable. She pulled her hands away from him and examined them herself.

Scorched skin peeled like ribbons from her fingertips, and her palms were covered with bloody gouges and splinters of glass. Her head started to spin, and the world was slipping away like paint dripping down a canvas.

"Grayson!" she heard Savvy yell. "Pull over!"

The truck came to a halt in front of Reuben Finch's log cabin. Gage reached for Nor, then everything faded to black.

When Nor came to, she was lying on a patch of grass along the side of the road. A rock dug into her shoulder blade. The clover beneath her head sank tiny claws into her scalp.

"Best thing is for me to get you all back up to the compound as soon as possible," said a voice.

"I don't think that'll be necessary," another voice hurried to say. "We can take ourselves." Almost as an afterthought, he added, "Sir."

"Suit yourself. But you know, son, you might not mind having someone between yourself and Dauphine Coldwater." Nor opened her eyes to see Reuben Finch standing over her, a heavy crease between his unruly eyebrows. "There she is. Welcome back."

A bright-blue braid tickled Nor's face. Savvy leaned in close and whispered, "Don't worry. You were only out for a few minutes. And you didn't puke."

"Great." Nor groaned. "Thanks."

"What do you say about getting up and inside?" Reuben asked.

Nor stood up woozily, and Reuben helped her into the house. It had a faint animal smell, both pungent and sweet, that Nor hadn't noticed the last time she'd been there. They passed through the kitchen and the living room with a large faded couch. Beside it, a framed picture of a little girl hung on the wall.

"All right, let's see what you've gotten yourself into now," Reuben said when they reached a washroom in the back of the house. He knelt in front of her. Nor looked away as he examined her ruined hands.

"These wounds look a lot like something I've treated on

your grandmother's hands a few times." He caught Nor's eye and chuckled. "Oh yes, I know all about you Blackburn women." He pulled a pair of surgical tweezers out of a cupboard above the sink. Nor stared at the way the sharp pointed end glinted in the light.

"Not much more I can do, I'm afraid," Reuben said after removing the splinters of glass from her hands. He turned on the faucet. "Run some cold water over your hands for a bit."

He set the tweezers by the sink and pulled a tin from the cupboard. "It's gonna hurt like all hell at first, but we'll put some of this on it. Should at least make the pain tolerable till we can get you to Judd."

Nor stuck her hands under the water. He was right. It hurt like hell. After a few minutes, she pulled her hands out, and Reuben gently patted a thick salve across her mangled palms. It smelled of vinegar. Nor's pain, hot like fire, dulled to a quiet roar.

"Funny thing though," Reuben said. "I don't recollect hearing that you shared Judd's talents." He stood. "Red here must be right. I must be getting old." The little fox waiting for him in the doorway gave an affectionate chirp and followed Reuben out of the room.

Nor had heard stories of how the pairing of a Blackburn daughter and her Burden might be made. Seeing Reuben with the little fox made Nor wonder if her Burden — her first Burden, that is — had come from her grandfather's natural gift with animals. Perhaps she was more connected to her grandfather than she had previously thought.

"He has a good point, you know," Gage said from the doorway. He'd wiped the blood from the side of his face. "I don't remember you being able to do a few things I saw today."

Shit, Nor thought. She stared down at her hands, the blisters glistening underneath the greasy balm. "I can explain —" she started.

Gage cut her off. "Since when did you start using black magic?"

"It's not black magic!" Nor insisted. "There are things I can do, and I can't explain why I can do them. I've tried to ignore them, but sometimes things just happen." Nor bit her lip to keep it from trembling. "But it's not black magic. I'm not my mother."

"I never said that you were."

Nor looked up, startled. "You believe me?"

"Why wouldn't I? You said sometimes it just happens. Like when?"

Nor thought back to when she'd fought off her mother's fern. She'd been scared then, just as much as she'd been when she saw Madge's hands wrapped around Gage's throat. And she was scared whenever she saw a lie. "I guess it mostly happens when I'm scared," she said.

"Have you ever healed anyone before?"

"A few times," she admitted. "I've never been able to do it on purpose before, though."

"And the scream?"

"I have no idea what that was."

"Sounded like the scream of a banshee." Gage nodded knowingly. "The last Blackburn able to harness that kind of power was Rona." He leaned against the doorframe. "So what else can you do?"

"Obviously nothing!" Nor blurted. "I couldn't save Madge. We barely got out of there alive. And as for that scream, I have *no fucking clue* where that came from and even less of a clue on how I could manage to do it again! *What else can I do?* I can't do *anything!*"

Gage stared at her. "And to think, I was almost impressed by you," he finally said humorlessly. "Word of advice? I wouldn't go showing just anyone what you can do. Not everyone is as open-minded as I am."

He left, and Nor swiped at her wet eyes, her old scars screaming so loudly she could barely hear anything else. According to the myths, a banshee's scream was an omen of death. The thought that, in this case, it could also be the cause of it was terrifying. She stared at those sharp tweezers on the edge of the sink. It would be so easy to just reach over, grab them, and hoard them in her pocket for later, when she was alone. She used to do that all the time. How many times had she waited until Apothia's back was turned to filch one of the steak knives from the wall? Nor's hand moved toward the tweezers. She watched her fingers close around them. She thought about Madge and all the ways she'd already failed today.

She hurled the tweezers across the room.

14

Concealment Spell

> "Just as one must recognize the time to stand and fight,
> one must also understand when it is better to hide
> and wait for the dawning of a new day."
> — Rona Blackburn

Pike and Sena Crowe leaped from the vehicle as soon as the yellow Jeep pulled up in front of Reuben's cabin. Pike was barely through the door when he grabbed Gage by the front of his shirt. "What the fuck, Gage? We told you to stay put."

"We handled it, okay?" Gage spat, struggling to free himself.

"Yeah, you handled it all right, cuz. A woman is dead, her business destroyed. Not to mention you put Nor at risk when it's our job to keep her safe."

"Wait, it's not his fault," Nor protested. "*I* was the one who —"

"No," Gage interrupted. "He's right. It was my idea." He looked at Pike. "You're just jealous you missed all the action."

"You're a real moron sometimes, you know that? I mean, I knew you were a dumb ass, but you put Nor — and *everyone else* — in danger today." Pike glanced at Nor and shook his head. "The fury the Giantess is going to rain down on you."

Before they left Reuben Finch's house, Nor took a last look at the picture of that little girl hanging on the wall. Neglect had clung to Nor like a bad smell back then.

On the drive back to the compound, she thought of the lumpy sweat-stained mattress she'd shared with her mother; she thought of how incense from the Witching Hour had filled her little room and made her cough. Mostly, however, she thought of Madge.

Madge hadn't grown tired of Nor the way Fern often did. Fern had delighted in Nor's presence one moment and then thought her a pest in the next, like a tiresome puppy. Children, like puppies, required care. Caring for something had never been Fern's strong suit. Fortunately for Nor, she'd had Madge.

Madge had given Nor a book of fairy tales for her eighth birthday and read to her sometimes before bed. Madge's favorite had been the story of a woman determined to rescue her child from the cold clutches of death. It was a story of self-sacrifice and unconditional love, but what Nor remembered most was the illustration of the poor woman crying her eyes out — her eyes literally dropping, like pearls, out of her head and into a great lake. The ending hadn't been a happy one.

If only Madge had figured out what Nor had: that a wish for a love like the kind found in fairy tales was a wish that should never be granted. Fairy tales were ugly and gruesome things. Like Rona had, Nor preferred the Greek myths. At least those were meant to be tragic.

When they reached the compound, they were met by a full-blown typhoon in the shape of Dauphine and Judd.

"In that head, underneath all that goddamn hair, is there a brain, girlie?" Judd bellowed, pounding her fist against Dauphine's table.

Nor slumped in her chair, eyes down. *Am I actually supposed to answer that?* she thought.

"And would you like that head to stay above ground," Judd continued, "or should I call Apothia and tell her to grab a shovel and start digging you a grave?"

"Now you wait just a minute," Dauphine interjected. Nor had to hand it to her. The woman barely reached Judd's midsection when standing, but she was a force to be reckoned with nonetheless. "If I know my grandchildren as well as I think I do, I'm going to assume Nor didn't act alone." And she pinned Gage with an icy glare before turning back to Judd. "For that, I assure you, there will be consequences."

Nor watched the color drain from Charlie's face.

"The girl's here now," said Everly, the man in the cowboy hat. "She's safe. And there's nowhere safer. Do we agree?" Judd nodded reluctantly. "Then it's settled," he determined, and leaned back in his chair. "We just need to make sure she stays here." He winked at Nor.

"It is certainly not settled," Judd boomed.

"Our family hasn't lost a Blackburn woman yet, and you know it," Everly huffed. "Though sometimes at the expense of one of our own." Gage's expression, Nor noted, had turned particularly steely at that comment.

"Judd is well aware of the sacrifices our family has made." Dauphine fixed her gaze on Nor's grandmother. "That said, Judd," she continued, "I think it's about time you stop being such a pain in my ass and let us do our job. Everly is right. You will *all* be safer up here with us."

Judd folded her arms across her chest. "Fine."

Dauphine jumped into action before Judd could change her mind. "Nor, you'll continue to stay here for the time being. Sena Crowe, please take the Oliveira boys, and —" She peered at Savvy through the jeweled spectacles balanced at the end of her nose. "I'm sorry, dear. I didn't catch your name?"

"Savannah Dawson," Savvy said with a small curtsy. "Guardian of Unwanted Things."

The corners of Dauphine's mouth twitched into a smile. "Sena Crowe, please escort the Oliveira boys and Savannah,

Guardian of Unwanted Things, next door. They can stay with you and Charlie for the night. And be sure to tell your mother I apologize for the inconvenience." She turned to Everly. "I take it you have the rest covered?"

"No one will get in *or* out of the compound without one of us knowing about it this time," Everly asserted. "I can guarantee that."

"As for the two of you," Dauphine said to Charlie and Gage, "clearly my reservations about allowing you to join your cousins were sound."

Gage opened his mouth to contest, and she held up a finger. "If I were you, I'd spend most of my time from this point on proving to me that you can be trusted, which will *not* be an easy task."

Gage and Charlie nodded solemnly, and Nor burned with shame. It had been her idea to leave the compound. She should have been the one taking the blame, but when she caught Gage's eye, he shook his head, and Nor kept her mouth shut.

Judd reached across the table and took Nor's hands in hers. "Now," Judd said, "I got more than a few things back home that need tending to. I'm going to trust that you'll stay put." She prodded at Nor's wounds. Some of the blisters had already crusted over. "You want to tell me what you got into this time?"

Nor considered telling her grandmother that she seemed to have inherited the healing touch, that Gage's pain had burned blisters into her skin. Gage had believed her, but what did he know? He'd never seen the effects of black magic like Nor and Judd had. What if Nor could do all these things because there was something bad in her? By telling Judd, she might be forcing her grandmother to confirm what Nor had always feared: that whatever rotten thing that was inside of Fern was inside of Nor as well.

"I'm not sure," Nor finally mumbled.

Judd grunted, and Nor tried not to glance at the purple cloud she'd sent floating into the air. Before she had time to gasp, her pain fell to the table as tiny ice crystals, and the wounds disappeared.

"This is exciting," Savvy said as Pike led them through the compound.

"Savvy," Nor chided, "you're staying because they think you'll be safer here than on the main part of the island. Doesn't that make you nervous? Don't you at least want to call and warn your dad?"

Savvy shrugged and flipped one of her long blue braids over her shoulder. "Nah. He's a tough old guy."

As they passed under the fountain, Savvy stopped to stare at the statue's impressive physique. "Her breasts are totally perfect," she said in awe, moving from one side of the fountain to the other. "Look at her nipples. Oh my God, they follow me wherever I go."

"Jealous?" Grayson teased.

Savvy rolled her eyes. "Please. That statue should be jealous of *me*."

"Oh yeah? About what exactly?" Grayson mocked, luridly sizing her up.

Savvy leaned in, as if she were about to share some great confidence with him. "My nipples are pierced," she said. The expression on Grayson's face was priceless.

"Um — when did you get your nipples pierced?" Nor asked after Grayson had pulled away.

"What? Oh, I didn't. I just wanted to shut him up."

Nor smiled. "I missed you."

Savvy hooked her arm through Nor's and grinned. "Right back atcha, babe."

Nor sighed before collapsing facedown onto the couch in Dauphine's basement. Bijou, who had been asleep on a pillow, grumbled in annoyance. "I'm sorry," Nor muttered.

Outside, a chilly rain had descended upon the island. Savvy was on the staircase, trying to flirt with Nor's new personal guard, whose job was apparently to follow Nor everywhere — even, to Nor's mortification, to the bathroom.

"Well?" Nor asked as soon as Savvy came into the room. Reed followed quietly behind her, and for one exasperating second, he was all she could see. *He's like gravity*, Nor thought. It didn't matter what else was going on. Looking at him, she understood why the tides were so captivated by the moon. It was ridiculous.

"Didn't even say hello," Savvy replied. Nor's new guard was far less agreeable than Pike; in fact, he made Sena Crowe look downright amiable. This guy wore a permanent scowl.

Savvy sighed dramatically and flopped down across the couch. "And I even brought him Red Vines!"

"That's not what I'm asking about, and you know it," Nor said.

"But don't worry," Savvy continued unnecessarily loudly. "I've got a plan. I'm bringing him gummy bears tomorrow." Satisfied, Savvy then leaned in close to Nor and whispered, "Okay, no idea when they're letting you out. You might have to plan on growing old down here. The only reason we were even able to come over is because we volunteered to get sleeping bags." She looked around the crowded basement with interest. "There's supposed to be a bunch down here somewhere."

"Be my guest," Nor said with a sigh. Savvy grinned, and they quickly lost her to the boxes and abandoned furniture piled everywhere.

Nor and Reed shared a small smile. Nor still couldn't believe he was here. After everything Reed had heard, every-thing he'd *seen*, no one would have blamed him for turning around and running for his life, never giving Nor another thought. But he hadn't.

That was something, wasn't it?

"I'm guessing you have a lot of questions," Nor said nervously.

"Savvy kind of filled me in," he admitted.

"So you know that I'm —"

"A witch?" He chuckled. "Yeah, I know." He brushed some hair away from her face. "But I already knew there was something special about you."

"I don't feel special." Nor glanced outside, noting that the storm had intensified. "I feel afraid," she admitted softly. Even if she tried, even if it mattered, she'd still lose. Hadn't she proven it by not being able to save Madge? Wasn't her skin covered with scars from every battle she'd ever fought and lost?

The room was suddenly lit by a bolt of lightning, and thunder crashed around them. The lights flickered. Savvy emerged from the other side of the room carrying three multicolored sleeping bags. A clock in the shape of a topless mermaid was tucked under one arm. "I cannot believe the amount of crap Dauphine has down here," she said wistfully. "This place is the stuff of dreams." She headed up the stairs, weighted by her bundle. "Don't worry, Nor," she called over her shoulder. "We will plan your escape from Azkaban tomorrow."

"Stay here," Nor begged Reed. "At least until you get kicked out."

As the rain beat against the windows, Reed wrapped his arms around her, brought his mouth to her collarbone, and lightly kissed her there. "For the record," he said before leaving, "I don't think being afraid is necessarily a bad thing. It means you're smart. Besides, being afraid doesn't seem to stop you. You're still here. You're still fighting. And I'm pretty sure that makes you the bravest person I know."

A few hours later, Nor's little room was lit by a solitary candle. Nor licked her finger and passed it over the flame. The flame danced. It was beautiful; so beautiful it was easy to forget that it could be dangerous as well. Or perhaps it seemed beautiful because it was dangerous. Just like the storm that raged outside her room. Just like her mother.

Nor blew out the candle and pulled the blankets up to her chin. Fern was just as frightening to her now as she'd been when Nor was a child. Could there be any truth to what Reed had said? Her skin was marked with scars, but maybe they didn't have to be reminders of all the times she'd let fear win, but rather of when she'd found the strength to keep fighting in spite of fear. Nor's eyes grew heavy and closed before she could answer herself.

Nor found herself standing in a bathroom of a derelict and abandoned hotel. The marble sink was slick with slime. The floor sparkled with shattered glass. The rain beat upon the dilapidated roof.

A faint sound, like that of a ripped seam, caught her attention. She looked down and watched with detached interest as the skin on her legs, as cracked as a dry river-bed, split open. Blood trickled to the floor. She grimaced in disgust.

They didn't heal, these wounds. Nor poked a red-taloned finger into a particularly deep and ugly gash on her arm, and then smeared the gore across the reflection in the tarnished, gilded mirror.

The skin on her mother's face was split, tiny black scabs on her cheeks looking like the cracks of a broken cup. She ran her fingers through her hair, and red strands floated to the floor.

She spat blood into the sink.

When she twisted on the bathtub faucet, the spigot coughed and sputtered before a trickle of brown water came out. When the tub was full enough, Nor slid into the cold, dirty water and raked her nails across the scabs on her body. Blood stained the muddy water pink.

Look at what she'd been reduced to. "And for what?" Nor rasped. There was no longer anything saccharine in that voice. Even her own gift — her delicious form of mind control — had waned.

She needed the girl. It had been her spilled blood that had brought him back in the first place, her sacrifice that had started it all. She looked more like him than ever. She also looked like Judd. She'd happily carve out any similarities the girl had to either. She just needed a way to get to her.

A bolt of lightning opened up the sky like a vein. Shortly

after, the horizon began to glow red with fire, and Nor saw a spectacle she'd never seen before. She didn't think there was anything but trees on that side of the island, but shadowy forms towered over the tree line. They were glaring at her with irksome, all-seeing eyes.

The fire spread and the sky grew brighter. Nor dug her fingertips into the nail bed of her opposite hand. Slowly, she pulled out her blackened nails, one by one, then dropped them to the bathroom floor.

Nor awoke with a start, the red of her mother's blood painted on the insides of her eyelids. Her cheeks burned as if from a fever. Heat licked the side of her body. The room was on fire.

Reanimation Spell

**"Do not forget that consciousness and
free will go hand in hand."**
— Rona Blackburn

The room was a pyre of heat and smoke and fire. The blaze crept up the window curtains, hissing and popping. Thick tongues of flames spread across the carpet. Only the couch remained untouched by the fiery assault, and Bijou stood at the end of it, barking angrily at the smoke edging around them, stalking its prey.

Terrified, Nor scooped up Bijou and leaped to the center of the room, the only spot free of flame. The blaze immediately engulfed the couch where she and Bijou had just been sleeping. If they were going to get out alive, she had no choice but to brave the inferno. She dashed straight through the fire and headed for the stairs. As she ran, the flames shrank from her; they evaporated like puffs of steam on contact. She didn't suffer a single burn. Her clothes were untouched, and Bijou's fur smelled only vaguely like smoke.

With her hair flying behind her and Bijou's wet nose tucked against her throat, Nor ran up the stairs past the body of a man lying slumped halfway up the steps, its skin black and raw. She plowed through the front door just as the windows of the basement exploded.

"Nor!" A screech rang out, and suddenly Nor was caught in a crushing embrace. "How in the hell are you not dead?" Savvy cried, gripping Nor's face with freezing hands. Savvy's tearstained face was smudged with soot, and there was a burn on her arm.

"Here," Nor said, pressing her hand against the burn. She felt a slight pinch, and the wound started to mend. Savvy stared at her arm in wonder.

"Have you seen Reed?" Nor asked. Savvy pointed across the compound, and Nor breathed a sigh of relief when she saw him, half-hidden by the statue of the woman with the bowl held over her head.

Nor turned back to the house. The fire was a raging monster, a black fire-breathing dragon scaling the roof and dropping burning shingles onto the crowd below. Some people were still in their pajamas. Others had obviously thrown on whatever clothes they could find; one man seemed to be wearing his wife's housecoat. Many of them were carrying buckets, vases, and watering cans to and from the fountain. Pike, Sena Crowe, and Gage stood knee-deep in the water. They couldn't fill the containers fast enough.

"What happened?" Nor asked.

"Lightning," Savvy said, sobbing. "It struck the house, and everyone else could get out, but they'd locked you in the fucking *basement*. Cliff went in after you."

"Cliff?"

"Your guard." Savvy sniffed. "The one who got you out." She ran her fingers through Nor's waist-long tresses and pulled away a handful of singed strands. "What did you do to your hair?"

Nor remembered the body on the basement stairs. She felt sick to her stomach. "Savvy, Cliff's dead."

"Cliff's dead?" Savvy wailed.

A whooshing crack filled the air as a great billowing cloud of fire erupted from the roof and spilled onto the neighboring houses. A woman screamed. Another bolt of lightning cracked purple across the blackened sky. Fiery ash rained down on the crowd, and soon everyone was covered in cinders, their faces contorted with so many different emotions. Fear. Grief. Defeat.

Nor set Bijou on the ground and splashed into the fountain. She had always thought that story about Rona and her wooden behemoths — the aegises, their protectors — had been a myth, a story elevated into legend by exaggeration. Nor pressed her hand against the wooden statue's leg.

At first, nothing happened.

And then, with a great creaking moan, the lady in the fountain turned her head and blinked at Nor with large, vacant eyes.

"Protect us," Nor breathed.

With a great rattle, the woman lifted her skirts and stepped out of the fountain, which sent Pike, Sena Crowe, and Gage scrambling and tripping to get out of her way. The crowd fell silent as the woman overturned her bowl of water onto the burning house.

"Holy shit!" Savvy gasped. "Nor, how did you do that? Never mind! It doesn't matter! Do the bear next! Or the cat!" Savvy dragged Nor around the compound, cheering as Nor brought all of the other statues to life, but stopped abruptly at the sculpture of the troll-like woman looming over the burning remains of Dauphine's house.

"Let's just skip this one," Savvy decided, backing away. "I don't think I'm ready to see that thing walking around just yet."

These are the things Nor would later remember: the utter magic of watching the inanimate come to life; the welcome feeling of relief that settled over the crowd; Savvy's incredulous laughter; Bijou's excited bark; and Charlie with her hands held out as the water the aegises poured over the flames fell like rain.

And then.

The clap of thunder was so loud that Nor almost believed she'd made it up. The lightning was so bright it looked like nothing at all. It was like staring at the sun, like watching the last sparks of a dying star. The tree it struck burst into flames, and suddenly something was on fire on either side of the compound.

The air turned black with smoke. Nor reached behind her and grappled for Savvy's hand. "Stay with me!" she yelled. The fire spread. It surged through the compound, crackling hot and bright and terrifying. Stumbling, they ran from the fast-moving blaze.

"We gotta get out of here!" she heard Gage shout.

Nor and Savvy now ran toward Gage's voice, dodging falling debris and the pounding feet of the aegises fighting the blaze: the bison, who gathered two crying children into a hooved embrace, gave a mighty flap of those thick, leathery wings and soared off into the night sky; the bear with his colossal ox horns; and the wolf, the quills on the back of his neck raised. The woman from the fountain emptied her bowl over one house and then another, dousing the flames. But not all of Rona's monsters were matches for the fire. First the wildcat faltered, and then the bear, his ox horns turning to cinders.

Nor and Savvy followed Gage away from the compound, away from the fire, and into the surrounding woods. The three fell to the ground and began coughing the smoke from their lungs. Charlie and Sena Crowe staggered in after them, carrying someone. It took Nor a second to realize who. It was Pike. The side of his face had been badly burned.

"Where's everyone else?" Nor coughed.

Charlie and Sena Crowe quickly lowered Pike to the ground. He lurched forward and retched, then his eyes rolled back and he started convulsing.

"Do something!" Gage yelled.

Nor could hear the others calling out for one another through the trees like lost children. She thought she heard Reed screaming her name over and over again, but she couldn't be sure.

"Try to keep him still," Nor said, her voice quivery. She placed her shaky hands on Pike's blistered cheek, but all she felt was a tiny pinch. She tried once more and still, nothing. Pike's breathing grew shallow.

"Nor," Savvy whimpered. "Help him."

He's going to die, Nor thought. *He's going to die, and everyone here will be forced to watch it happen.* "I'm trying!" she choked. *I'm afraid, but I'm trying.*

Nor gritted her teeth and pressed her hands harder against the burn until Pike's pain finally trickled out, as slowly as an intravenous drip, onto the ash-covered ground. The wound struggled to knit itself back together, a scar like a jellyfish sting spreading across Pike's cheek. Finally, his breathing steadied.

Nor fell back on her heels with relief, her heart pounding wildly. She looked around at the small band of survivors.

Gage's arms were bright red from the fire's wrathful touch. A deep gash ran along Savvy's face. Sena Crowe's shirt was ripped. Charlie's arms were scratched and bloody. But Nor? Nor had run through a burning building, and all that she had lost was some hair.

All around them, the woods glowed the hazy orange of a dying fire and were filled with the sounds of people calling out, trying to find one another in the chaos and the dark. She wondered where Reed was. Grayson. Bijou.

Nor went to stand, but Gage quickly pulled her back down. "What the hell are you doing—?" she began, but what she saw next stopped her cold.

If it hadn't been for the light of the flames, she might have mistaken them for people. There were at least a dozen of them. Slinking out from behind the trees, with their gray, rotting skin and their blackened eyes and tongues, they looked like monsters, like nightmares.

The Resurrected. And they were heading straight for Nor and the others.

"I thought you said the compound was undetectable," Nor whispered. She recognized many of the faces under dead gray features. One of them had once been Bliss Sweeney. Another had been the boy with the Mohawk, the one who had helped Catriona bring Wintersweet to Fern. These were fellow islanders, people whose loved ones had laid them to rest in Anathema Island's cemetery. Had Nor's mother been the reason for all those graves? Is that why they were here?

Had they been brought back to life only to be used to carry out Fern Blackburn's commands?

"It is," Charlie answered shakily. "Or at least, it was."

She brandished her dagger at one of the Resurrected, looming menacingly over Pike's prone body. Gage pushed Nor behind him.

"They're here for me," Nor said to Gage.

"They're not getting you," he grunted, wielding the knife clutched in his hand.

But a sharp object meant nothing to the dead. One grabbed hold of Savvy's blue braids and yanked her to the ground. Sena Crowe lunged at it with his knife, but the blade sank right through its dead gray skin like it was slicing into rotten fruit. Black sludge leaked out of the wound and onto the ground. Savvy whimpered as the creature swiped its blackened tongue across her cheek. Scared tears spilled down her cheeks.

Nor had become all too familiar with fear. Too many times it had coated Nor's insides black and filled her throat with its bile. Too often it marked the faces in her dreams and nightmares: Wintersweet right before a fern had wrapped itself around her throat. Bliss Sweeney right before she'd been killed.

In anger, Nor pulled away from Gage. "Let her go," she commanded, speaking to the Resurrected that was terrorizing Savvy.

"Nor, what the hell are you doing?" Gage hissed.

I'm not sure, Nor thought to herself. But if her unexpected and unbidden gifts were any sign, she might be able to do something. She had to take that chance.

"I'll come with you," she said to the Resurrected. "I'm the one she wants." The one clutching Savvy's hair loosened its grip. It turned toward Nor, staring at her with its black dead eyes. She had piqued their interest. Savvy took a tentative step back toward Sena Crowe — and then the ground began to quake.

Once. Twice. Three times.

The lady from the fountain had come to stand in front of Nor, to use her giant bowl to shield Nor. Her thunderous arrival knocked Nor to the ground, and she brought the overturned bowl down over Nor to trap her there. Nor's face skidded against the rocks and dirt.

"Savvy!" Nor cried. Nor rolled over and beat her hands and feet against the top of the bowl. It was no use. The shield wouldn't budge.

From under the bowl, she could hear screaming and the sound of people running. And then she heard nothing but her own ragged breath, her own pulse drumming in her ears.

Finally the statue lifted the bowl a bit and peered in at Nor.

"Let me go," Nor commanded in a voice so irate and so determined, she hardly recognized it as her own. With reluctance, the aegis lifted the bowl completely, setting Nor free.

Nor scrambled out, slipping on wet leaves and muddy ashes. Pike, still unconscious, lay a few yards away. Charlie was beside him, one cheek sliced open, one leg bent at an odd angle. Before Nor had a chance to go to her, Gage came crashing toward her through the trees.

"They took Savvy," he said, panting. "Those ghouls, or whatever they were. Sena Crowe, too."

Nor closed her eyes and thought of her best friend, beaten and bloody and afraid. Nor could hear Savvy's screams so clearly in her head it was as if she hadn't stopped screaming. Maybe she hadn't. "I'm going after them."

"If you were right that they came for you," Gage said, "that your mother just wants *you*, then this is probably a trap."

"All the more reason for me to go," Nor said. "She'll kill them if I don't. You know she will." She looked at Gage, expecting him to try to dissuade her.

But all he said was, "I'm in."

Nor looked back at Charlie uncertainly. How could she leave her and Pike to fend for themselves?

"What are you waiting for?" Charlie barked, giving Nor her answer. "Go!"

Gage and Nor took off toward the woods. On the way, Nor spotted Reed, standing on the other side of the compound where only a few flames still burned. He had Bijou cradled in one arm and the other wrapped around Grayson's shoulder protectively. The look on Reed's face was one of bewilderment and disorientation, and Nor was struck with guilt and remorse.

She had brought him — and everyone else around her — nothing but terror and pain.

But that stopped now. Nor darted after Gage.

The aegises shuffled back to their posts and stiffened into lifeless statues once more, the face of the woman in the fountain turned forlornly toward where Nor had disappeared into the trees.

Gage and Nor made their way down a curved trail in the woods. With every step, Nor could feel the sheathed knife Charlie had insisting on sliding into the side of her boot. The saphenous vein in Nor's ankle pulsed against it; the mere possibility of spilled blood had woken it up.

The trail Nor and Gage were on had been familiar once, but as the woods were now, Nor didn't recognize it at all. The trees were warped like deformed skeletons. Black moss dripped from branches like mourning veils. Instead of the distant cascade of Lilting Falls, she heard a sound like a dull grinding, as if someone were wading through miles of broken glass. And when the lake came into view, Nor saw why.

"Holy shit," she breathed.

Celestial Lake had turned to ice. A wall of ice, to be exact. A wall that stood as high as a grown man's hip. It crept its eerie way toward shore, and as it went it sprouted thin crystal fingers that groped at whatever was in its path. It reminded Nor of the mythical River Styx and the desperate hands of the damned reaching, pleading for salvation in the wake of Charon's ferry.

Nor and Gage inched their way around the lake, whose icy limbs twitched like the whiskers on a sleeping beast. It raged with a kind of vengeance that made Nor uneasy.

"Is this because of your mother?" Gage shouted to Nor.

Nor shook her head. "No," she said. "I think it's because of *me*." The hostile plants, that eerie fog, the sudden lightning storm, all brought to mind the way the body's immune system, in its desperation to destroy an invading virus, could go so far as to destroy itself. Was it possible that Nor's fear — of her mother, of *herself* — had grown so large that she'd infected the entire island with it?

Nor shuddered when the wall of ice swept over a maple tree as if it were nothing more than a blade of beach grass.

And now it might be too late. The island, she realized, might no longer care who it had to fight off.

It might just destroy them all in its desperate attempt to save itself.

16

Healing Spell

*"One should always hope for blood; with blood comes
a wound one can reasonably hope to repair."*
— Rona Blackburn

The air out on the ocean stung, cold and merciless. Nor
could barely feel the tips of her fingers. After turning her
face away from the wind, she wiped strands of wet hair
from her cheek and looked back at Anathema Island. All she
could see of it was the aegises looking out across a haze of
smoke.

Gage pulled the skiff up to the dock at Halcyon Island.
Like the rest of Halcyon, the marina was quiet and empty;
only a small dinghy remained afloat. The rest of the boats
had sunk and stuck out of the water at odd angles, like sinking graves in an abandoned cemetery.

"You sure this is it?" he asked.

Nor nodded. Before them loomed the abandoned hotel,

the quintessential witch's castle in a dark and twisted fairy tale.

"Then I think we both know why that body was found here last fall," Gage said. He paused to stare at the limp rope in his hand, trying to decide if more pain would come from hoping to live or from preparing to die. "You know," he said, "there's no guarantee we'll get back to Anathema."

Nor ripped the rope from his hand and wrapped it around the post. "Quit being so damned dramatic," she said, as if saying so would quiet the sound of her own hammering heart.

They climbed the steps of the marina and had to fight their way through a thicket of fast-growing thistles. They had barely made it to the top when the entire stairway was swallowed by it, and a vine even shot out and grabbed Nor's ankle. She dug at it with her fingers but couldn't break its hold. With effort, she pulled out the knife wedged in her boot and hacked at the vine.

It yelped, let go of Nor's leg, and dragged itself back into the carpet of foliage choking the dock. Nor tossed the knife onto the ground and bounded after Gage, the plant's screams echoing in her ears.

They found their way into the hotel's open courtyard. There, a bonfire raged. At first, Nor thought it was lawn furniture that was burning.

"Bones," Gage said flatly. He was right: a pile of bones stacked and lit like sticks and branches.

Nor was quite certain they were the bones of the Resurrected. The Resurrection Spell didn't last very long, and the only thing to do once the spell had worn off was to burn the undead.

Vines covered the old hotel's stone facade, and most of the windows were broken. "You should stay out here," Nor suggested.

Gage rolled his eyes. "Now who's being dramatic?"

Except for a few disemboweled couches, the lobby inside was empty. A chandelier hanging in the center of the round room swung eerily, and the mirror behind the lobby desk was shattered. The walls were covered in crude graffiti.

They crept up the stairs leading to the second floor. Suddenly the staircase rocked and bucked. Nor lost her balance and started to fall, but Gage caught her. He wrapped his arms around her, bracing them for another quake. Nor felt the wild beat of his heart against her back. The tremor lasted only a moment, and then, with the world steady once more, Nor pulled away from Gage.

They took the stairs two at time. At the end of a long hallway, an ornate door was marred with carved gashes. They walked down the hallway, wondering if they'd find someone on the other side of that door.

The room had been meant for happy occasions: weddings, formal dinners, cocktail parties. It had once been decorated with large waving palm trees, and the walls had been covered in tiles the color of rich jewels, reminiscent of a Turkish bath. Only bits and pieces of those palm trees and brightly colored tiles remained and were scattered across the floor.

The few people inside the room moved as if drugged. One writhed across the floor. Another looked like a robotic toy whose batteries were running out. A woman stared into a piece of cracked mirror she held in her hand, transfixed by her skeletal reflection. Next to her, a man walked into a wall again and again on a permanent repeat. A low moaning filled the room: the sound of despair and desolation.

From out of a darkened corner stepped Fern, tattoos unfurling sensuously from her porcelain skin. They rose and arced over her head, like Medusa's hair of snakes. Nor and her mother locked eyes. The ferns retracted, whipping through the air with a snap.

"Nor," Fern crooned, putting on a honeyed smile. "I am so glad you came to see me." Fern moved closer, followed by Catriona. Nothing was left of the jovial girl who used to sell fish at the farmers' market on Saturday mornings. A scarf covered her face, but did little to hide the angry red tattoos that spread across her cheeks and forehead.

Nor caught a glimpse of her own reflection in the fragmented mirror on the back wall and almost gasped. She and her mother couldn't have looked more different from each other right then. Nor was still wearing the clothes she'd worn to bed. They were ripped and covered in dirt and blood. Her hair — what was left of it — was a wild halo around her head. Her face was plain. She was just a kid. Fern's glamorous red hair cascaded down over her shoulders. She was wearing a high-collared green dress, more sheath than gown, slit from ankle to thigh; a long black silk glove concealed her left hand and arm. The other arm was wrapped in deadly but gorgeous green tattoos.

But when Nor took a closer look at her wickedly beautiful mother, she observed chinks in her armor: thin black scabs on her cheeks, dark-red stains on her dress, tufts of hair missing from her scalp, dried blood clinging to her ankles, and on her calves, a lattice of fresh wounds.

"What did you do with my friends?" Nor demanded.

Fern sneered. "Oh, *them*. I don't want to talk about *them* just yet. Instead, I'm going to tell you a story." Her tattoos reached out again toward Nor, like pythons taking the measure of their victim. They sizzled when they got too close, and recoiled.

"Once upon a time," Fern said, her voice still sickly sweet, "a beautiful witch fell in love with a prince. Sadly, the charming prince didn't return the witch's affections. So she tried casting a spell. At first, the spell didn't work. She tried again and again, and eventually stumbled upon the secret for casting any spell — for fortune, fame, power, even spells to raise the dead; spells no Blackburn daughter had attempted since Rona herself. To work, the spells needed a blood sacrifice, and — this is my favorite part — the blood had to be the blood of someone from Anathema Island." She paused.

"Well, that's not completely true. The spell will still work, just not as well. Plus, it's more fun to kill people you know."

"You're talking about black magic," Nor said.

Fern's eyes flashed in anger. "I'm talking about magic that is rightfully mine as a Blackburn. The kind of magic that should have been giving me everything I've ever wanted. The kind of magic that I was forced to take for myself!" Fern pointed at the young woman staring at herself in the mirror. "What would you do if I killed her, Nor?" she asked, as if killing someone would be as simple as wiping lipstick from the rim of a wineglass. She laughed, a cackle that raised the hairs on the back of Nor's neck. Nor imagined the woman's head breaking open under her mother's pointed heel.

"My friends," Nor said through gritted teeth. "Where are they?"

Fern ignored her. "Would you try to save her, like you tried to save Madge? The woman utterly betrayed you, and still you tried to save her life." Fern clucked her tongue. "Pathetic."

"If you've hurt Savvy —" Nor blurted angrily.

Fern gritted her teeth. "Every hair on your friends' heads — blue or otherwise — is intact. They may have received a few injuries on the way here, but some things just can't be helped."

Gage narrowed his eyes at Fern. "So if you weren't planning on sacrificing them, what was the point of taking them?" he asked.

Fern leaned toward them, and Nor could smell her mother's breath, equal parts sweet and rancid. "You're here, aren't you? And you're afraid, aren't you? When people are afraid, they are very easy to control." Suddenly, Fern pointed to the woman at the mirror and barked, "Kill her."

The zombies around them were instantly animated. They descended upon the woman like animals, clawing, biting, and tearing. The woman's screams were quickly silenced.

The carnage over, Fern's assassins drifted away, except for one who stayed to lick a last splash of blood from the floor.

"Are you afraid yet, Nor?"

Before Nor could respond, she heard the nauseating crunch of breaking bones. Catriona had reached over and taken Gage's hand in hers, squeezing it until Gage fell to the ground with a cry of pain. Catriona ripped the knife from his broken fingers and then trapped his hand under her foot.

Catriona passed the knife to Fern, who used it to force Nor to her knees. "You can't possibly think you're as strong as I am, can you? Do you really think you can beat me?" She laughed. "Let's play a little game then and see. It's called, 'I'm going to kill all your friends,' starting with that pretty blue-haired thing I have locked in the basement. And then this silly little boy here," she said, nodding toward Gage. "Not that he'll be much of a challenge." Gage trembled with fury.

"And then I think I'll kill Judd. And Apothia." Her eyes greedy with bloodlust, Fern held the sharp edge of the knife against Nor's jaw. "I'm going to kill them all, Nor, because I want to and there's nothing you'll be able to do to stop me because you'll already be dead."

Fern pressed the knife into Nor's skin and dragged it heavily along her jaw and across her cheek. Nor held her breath, waiting for the sting of the blade and the warm, wet blood to follow. Instead, she watched, dumbstruck, as a thin red line materialized on her mother's face instead.

Fern narrowed her eyes and looked at Nor with some uncertainty. She touched her cheek, then pulled away fingers red with blood. Nor reached up to touch her own face. It was as if the knife had never touched her.

In a fury, Fern grabbed Nor by the hair, yanked her head to the side, and tried to slit Nor's throat. Blood spurted instead from a wound that opened on her own neck. With an angry shriek, Fern lunged at Nor and scratched her with talon-like nails until her own cheeks were covered in gruesome claw marks. She brought her teeth down on Nor's shoulder, and a bite mark appeared on her own. Fern stabbed at Nor with the knife again and again until, exhausted and blood-soaked, she fell to the ground.

Nor almost tripped over her mother as she scrambled back toward Gage.

Catriona moved to help Fern, but Fern swatted her away,

leaving three red welts on Catriona's arm. "Take them downstairs with the others," she ordered. She coughed and spit a blackened tooth into her hand. "Go!" she sputtered.

Nor let herself be hauled away. Fern's blood continued to spread across the floor.

Catriona dragged Gage and Nor deep into the entrails of the hotel, passing through one darkened hallway after another. Gage cradled his injured hand. Catriona raked her jagged nails across the graffitied stone walls as they walked, eyeing Nor suspiciously all the while.

Mutely, Catriona pointed them down a winding stairwell. The scarf wrapped around her face slipped momentarily, and before she could adjust it, Nor caught a glimpse of what Catriona had really been hiding behind that veil: Fern had cut out her tongue.

Nor closed her eyes in horror. Was there anything Fern hadn't taken from this girl? Was there anything Catriona wouldn't give Fern? Nor wondered if there was any point in trying to appeal to the Catriona she once knew. That person had probably been erased long ago.

The stairs ended at a long, dark grotto littered with hollow wine barrels and broken bottles. She recognized this place from her dreams. She was almost certain that if she looked down, she'd see Bliss Sweeney's blood staining the stone floor.

The only light in the grotto came from the tiniest sliver

of moon shining through a small window high above their heads.

A blue blur darted out from one of the shadowy corners and threw itself at Nor.

"I knew you'd come!" Savvy cried. "Didn't I say they would, Sena Crowe?"

"Yup." Sena Crowe was slumped against the back wall of the alcove. He had a nasty cut on his face.

Nor hugged Savvy. "Are you okay?" she asked.

"If by okay you mean will I have nightmares for the rest of my life and will I need loads of therapy to function in normal society, then yeah." Savvy smiled. "Never better."

"What is this place?"

"Pretty sure it was the wine-tasting cellar," Savvy answered. She kicked at a few empty bottles, and they rolled across the floor with a loud clatter. "Please tell me you have a plan for getting us out of here. Sena Crowe is far too pretty to die in a wine cellar turned torture chamber."

"No one's going to die," Gage said.

But, as if on cue, the ground trembled again. Nor stumbled and grabbed at Gage's hand to steady herself. The moment their hands touched, she felt a sharp zap like an electric shock. Nor quickly pulled her hand away, but smoke poured from her fingertips, and the bones in Gage's hand were mended.

The ground stopped shaking. Gage flexed his newly healed fingers.

"We don't have a plan," she murmured.

"Did we ever? I'm guessing the only plan you had," he countered quietly, "was offering yourself up as a sacrifice in the hope that she'd let the rest of us go."

Nor smiled in spite of herself. "I guess it wasn't a great plan," she admitted.

"It was a terrible plan," he agreed. "It also didn't account for one very important thing."

"What's that?"

"That I wouldn't let you do that," he said softly. "I can't risk losing you." Gage cleared his throat, and if it weren't so dark, Nor was certain she'd see his face turning red. "What I mean by that," he was quick to clarify, "is that none of us can."

Again the floor swayed beneath their feet. Empty wine bottles rolled from one end of the room to the other. "Unfortunately," Gage said, "there's a pretty good chance the only defense that we've got left against your mother is you."

The ground continued to shake sporadically throughout the night. Water dripped steadily down the walls. A shallow pool of water skimmed the floor. Next to her Savvy shivered and huddled closer to Nor for warmth.

Through the moon's faint light, Nor could just make out the hazy outline of Savvy's profile, the ethereal glow of her unraveling blue braids. Someone else shifted uncomfortably on the floor, but no one had said much of anything for a while. Either a disquieting resignation had settled over the room, or perhaps they'd simply fallen asleep.

Nor thought of her mother's malicious ferns. How easily they could hurt Savvy and Sena Crowe and even Gage. But they hadn't been able to hurt Nor.

And apparently neither could Fern.

If Gage was right — if she was the last line of defense between Fern and everyone else — she still didn't know how that would help her protect them. When it came to her mother, she'd only just discovered that she could protect *herself.*

17

Vanishing Spell

"Fair warning: those who disappear rarely return."
— Rona Blackburn

Nor hadn't thought it possible to fall asleep in that cold, dark room, but she must have because the next time she opened her eyes it was to the shrill sound of voices and the pounding of frantic running overhead. A cascade of water spilled down one of the walls; it bubbled up between the cracks in the stone floor. A man was leaning over her, his face obscured by the flashlight he shined in her eyes.

Nor jumped to her feet. The man drew the light away. "Come on," he said, motioning for Nor and the others to follow him. "We need to get you out of here."

Gage gave Nor a look. *Should we trust him?* he asked

with his eyes, but Nor was too distracted by the man to pay much attention to anything else.

"Hey," Savvy said, gently shaking Nor's shoulder. "Who is this guy?"

He had three long scratches, like claw marks, across his cheek, and his eyes were the same gray-blue she saw when she looked in the mirror. "I think he's my father," Nor said quietly.

Savvy looked at her with widened eyes. "No shit," she breathed.

"We don't have a lot of time," Quinn Sweeney said urgently. "This place is going to be nothing but ashes by dawn."

Gage reached down and took Nor's hand. "Let's go," he said quietly. Nor nodded mutely. Of all the things that might have happened here, she'd certainly never expected to find him. *Father.* Even the word itself felt foreign.

They followed Quinn Sweeney up the winding staircase, their feet splashing through water that had already risen over the first few bottom steps. At the top of the stairs, they paused to let him catch his breath. He coughed wetly into a handkerchief. A splatter of blood stained the white linen.

They were standing in what, many years before, must have served as the Halcyon family's dining room. As it was now, nothing was left to suggest that the room had ever been grand. A stained and moldy mattress lay on the floor. A thick layer of dust and debris covered everything but the broken grand piano in the far corner of the room. Quinn dropped tiredly onto the piano bench and ran his fingers across the out-of-tune keys.

A gust of wind blew in through the broken window. It whipped Savvy's blue braids back and forth like flags caught in a storm.

"So what's the plan?" Gage asked. "How do we get out of here?"

"Out?" Quinn gave an empty laugh. "There is no getting out. Trust me, I've tried every possible escape route there is out of this hellhole."

A feeling of dread washed over Nor: the only door that led to the rest of the hotel had been boarded and nailed shut. "What do you mean?" she asked warily.

"I'm sorry. I didn't mean to make you think escaping was possible," Quinn said. "I'm afraid all I've done is delayed the inevitable for you. Your mother's power may be waning, but that hasn't made her any less dangerous. If we try to escape, she'll only kill you, and whatever death she has in store for you will be far worse than anything you'll experience down here."

A surge of water suddenly gushed up from the cellar. Savvy scrambled onto Gage's back. Sena Crowe splashed across the room and attempted to kick down the door. But it was no use.

"Your mother has killed just about everyone else. I didn't think any of us who are left would want to die alone." Quinn watched the water rise with indifference. "You know, at first

I thought we'd die in a fiery blaze; instead we'll drown. I find that comforting. I've never much liked fire."

The water was rising so fast Nor couldn't keep her balance. She toppled over and landed with a splash, banging the side of her hip painfully against the floor and planting her hand on a shard of broken glass. Outside, the wind screamed and howled. The sky had turned a hopeless black.

"She won't kill me, but at least now she won't be able to kill you *because* of me." He hesitated, then said, "Like she killed my mother and so many people before her."

Nor looked at Savvy, who was trying to stay on Gage's shoulders as the icy water inched higher. Sena Crowe was turning his shoulder black and blue by throwing himself against the door again and again.

"There's no point," Quinn called. "Even if you do escape, Fern will kill anyone left here if she thinks it might bring back her power. She will make it rain fire. She will make the earth split open and swallow us whole."

Nor pulled the shard of glass from her palm. She stood and walked quickly through the water. It was painfully cold. The closer it got to her chest, the harder it got to breathe. *Where is it all coming from?*

She nudged Sena Crowe away from the door. After wedging her fingers behind one of the boards nailed across it, she pulled until she felt the wood give and crack. Splinters pierced the soft flesh under her nails. One by one, she ripped the boards away from the door and tossed them into the water while the others watched, dumbstruck.

"Go!" she sputtered. Gage hoisted Savvy higher onto his back. The water circled them like a beast. Though there wasn't a hint of weariness in his face, Nor could see that it took everything Gage had to keep himself and Savvy from being swept away. With Sena Crowe's help, he managed to get through the doorway. Sena Crowe stepped through after them.

"Nor!" Gage yelled. "Come on!"

The water had risen to her collarbone. If it rose any higher, she wouldn't be able to keep her feet on the floor. Some water splashed into her mouth, and it had a metallic taste, like limestone or granite. Or blood.

Nor looked back at the piano, where her father had been sitting. He was gone. She swam to the piano and groped around under the water until she found her father's wrist and pulled. "Don't do this!" she cried when he surfaced.

"Nor, please," he sputtered. "Do you have any idea what it's like? A few weeks ago, your mother's power started to weaken, and I woke up and found years of my life suddenly gone, vanished without a trace or a memory. I found loved ones buried, dreams long dead. Let me go. Please."

Nor tried to imagine what it was like to drown. Perhaps it was peaceful, as if all you had to do was surrender and let death wash over you, like watercolor paint saturating a piece of paper.

Or maybe it was something else entirely. Perhaps a death

by drowning was eerily quiet because the water had stolen your voice. To scream, you had to be able to breathe. Under that serene facade was violence. Under that mask of apathy was terror.

"Let me be free of this hell," he begged.

Nor looked into his pleading eyes. With quiet irony, she noted that out of all the things Fern had told her about her father, she'd never mentioned that Nor had his eyes. "Not like this," she said.

Mara, the third Blackburn daughter, wasn't spoken of very often. This was most likely because her Burden had terrified the fellow islanders.

Mara's mental capacity and disposition had never evolved beyond those of a child, a sweet child who could hold death in her hands as gently as a flower. And like a bouquet, she'd gifted death to ailing neighbors and eased them peacefully into the afterlife. For those in agony, Mara's Burden was truly a blessing, a gift of mercy. For the mourners left behind, it was more difficult to view it that way. Their lack of appreciation and understanding became clear when sweet Mara was found floating facedown in the waters of Celestial Lake.

No record existed of exactly *how* this wide-eyed Angel of Death had aided her neighbors' passings, and Mara wasn't known to be a particularly communicative or intelligible young woman.

As Nor leaned over Quinn Sweeney, however, she instinctively knew exactly what Mara had done. Tenderly, Nor leaned over her father as if to kiss him farewell and filled her lungs with his last breath, like sipping air through a straw. Then she let him go, and the water slowly pulled him under. The serenity in Quinn Sweeney's handsome face told Nor with utter clarity that at least in death, her father had finally found some peace.

Nor waded through the doorway and down a hallway. At the end of the hall, she climbed a flight of stairs that was still just beyond the water's icy reach. It wouldn't be long, though, before it reached up here, too. Suddenly Nor couldn't stop shaking. What had happened to the other people in the hotel? Had her mother really killed all of them? Or had they, like her father, simply given up first?

"Well, that sucked," Savvy said when Nor caught up with them. She shivered and pushed strands of wet blue hair off of her face. Sena Crowe helped her to her feet.

Gage pointed out a window. Nor could see Charlie's skiff rocking up and down on the restless waves, a tiny beacon of hope. "Thanks to you," Gage said, "we might actually be able to get out of here." Instead of making Nor feel better, though, it made her feel worse. Every step they took to reach that boat would be a fight. And even then, there was no guarantee they'd make it back to Anathema in the storm. *All thanks to me.*

The sky was so dark it was as if someone had extinguished

the stars, had wrapped the moon in a shroud and buried it deep underground. The rain pounded against the window.

"You should go," Nor said to the other three. "Before the storm gets any worse."

"What about you?" Savvy protested.

"Someone needs to stop my mother."

"Nor . . ." Gage said quietly, shaking his head. He looked at her and that was when Nor realized that, until now, she'd never seen him afraid. She put her arms around him. He froze, and then he slid his hands around her waist and pulled her closer to him.

"I want to say you'll be okay," he said quietly, "but I'm not sure if that's true."

"I'm not, either," she whispered back. His hands moved up into her wet hair, and for a mere fraction of a second, Nor pressed her lips against his.

"I'll go with you," he murmured.

"No." She pulled away and saw she'd left a smear of her blood on his neck. "Get the others home. Keep them safe."

Nor squeezed her fingers together into a fist, and blood bubbled up through the gash in her palm. There wasn't time to stay and argue. There wasn't time for her to do anything now but to keep going up — to the roof where she was certain to find her mother pouring her wrath down on the rest of the world like the blood from so many wounds.

But that was the thing: Nor had stopped being afraid of blood a long time ago.

* * *

Nor pounded up the stairs to the hotel's roof. She reached the door and pushed her way into the gale. The storm nearly knocked her back inside.

Fern had her back turned. A black veil was wrapped around her head. "Did you think you had beaten me?" she called to Nor. "Did you think you'd be lucky enough to defeat *me?*" She turned then. The black veil whipped in the wind like a wild animal. She finally looked like the harbinger of death and destruction that she was. Another roof. Another night of darkness and blood, of pain and anguish, like the one Nor remembered as a neglected little girl.

"Tell me, daughter," Fern asked darkly, "do I seem defeated to you?"

She lurched at Nor and grabbed her by the shoulders. "Look at me!" Fern screamed. "Even the almighty Rona Blackburn would bow before me. She would tremble at my feet! I can bring the dead to life. I summon the shadows, and the shadows come! I am Hecate, Goddess of Storms, Lady of the Underworld, Enemy of Mankind. I am doom and death, misery and blame! I am the thing even the darkness fears!"

Fern's tattoos crept across her skin like barbed wire or broken capillaries. Blood seeped from wounds crisscrossing her skin and trickled onto the wet roof. Her head and neck were squeezed into an unnatural shape by tight black vines.

"Then what does that make me?" Nor asked.

"You?" Fern cackled. "You are *nothing*! You are *no one*!"

Blood dripped from Nor's injured hand. It mingled with her mother's blood on the wet roof until it was just one dark red stream.

"But you said it yourself. I'm *your* daughter," Nor said, raising her voice above the howling winds. The storm raged with renewed fury. Fern took a step back. She screeched when the wind tore a ribbon of skin from her cheek. Then another from her arm.

"I am Hecate," Fern wheezed, "Goddess of Storms." Her voice whistled through the holes in her face.

"That may be true," Nor cried. "You may be doom and death, misery and blame, but none of those things frighten me. *I* know what misery is. *I* know what blame is. There is no pain that you can cause that I haven't already felt."

Another strip of skin was ripped from Fern's cheek and carried off by the wind. She shrieked in confusion.

Nor started to laugh. "Don't you understand?" she screamed. "Death and I are now friends! And you can't hurt me or anyone else ever again. *I* won't let you."

The sky above them had become a black hole, an insatiable beast with its mouth open wide in a cry of terrible torment. Fern fell to her knees as her skin cracked and flaked like ancient porcelain. "I am the thing that the darkness fears!" she croaked before her jaw unhinged and fell away. Nor closed her eyes, preparing for the black sky to swallow her and her mother whole.

But then a memory pierced the darkness. Warm yellow light flowed through Nor's palms as she remembered another glow, growing larger and larger until she recognized it as the lit bowl of a pipe: the pipe of her grandmother, who had spent all that time quietly waiting for her to return home. Nor pictured Apothia's smile and recalled Savvy's laugh. She remembered the feel of Reed's hands on her skin, Bijou's happy dreams, and the fact that alpacas hummed when they were content. She pictured Gage, battling those storming seas below, and her scars, evidence of all the times she'd battled death before and won. Nor held out her brilliant shining hands, and their light vanquished the shadows and black holes that surrounded them.

The rains stopped, the clouds broke, and the moon reappeared in a night sky no longer beastly with rage. The winds ceased howling. The ocean calmed.

"You're wrong, Mother," Nor said quietly. "*I* am the thing the darkness fears."

And the rest of Fern Blackburn, unfurled like a spool of frayed ribbon, was swept up by the wind and hurled into the sky.

Illumination Spell

"Even the darkest of nights will come to an end."
—Rona Blackburn

When Nor arrived back on Anathema Island, she wasn't sure if whole days had gone by or merely hours. Sunlight sparkled off the water, and the ocean lapped softly against the shore. Nor tied up the dinghy, grateful the old boat had managed to stay afloat.

The island's plant life seemed to be recovering. New buds and leaves bloomed where once there had been only thorns. For Nor, however, it wouldn't be that easy. No amount of soaking her clothes would ever completely lift away the stains of her mother's blood, her own blood, the blood of her friends. Some things could not — would not — be washed away.

Nor made her way down Meandering Lane and stopped at the island's small cemetery. Kikimora, the cat, was sitting outside the black iron fence. She stared at Nor and then padded through the open gate. Nor followed.

Most of the graves were old, their epitaphs worn smooth with age. Nor walked to Rona's headstone. Though there had always been much speculation surrounding Rona's death, the truth was that she had died of natural causes. According to the diary she kept, Rona never cast another spell after her daughter, Hester, was born. Perhaps out of guilt, or perhaps she'd simply had enough of the magic in her blood. Nor wondered if peace was something that she, burdened with so many "gifts," could one day find as well.

Nor found a small piece of cedar plank on the ground. Using her fingernail, she roughly carved Madge's name into the soft wood. After examining her work, she propped it up against Mara's headstone and followed Kikimora back out onto Meandering Lane.

That evening Nor stood on the Tower's front porch. Kikimora sat beside her watching the silvery flicker of fish swimming in a pond the storm had left in the front yard. The limbs of the apple trees hung upside down, like broken fingers; the pebbled walk that had once shone like a stream of molten lava was scattered across the lawn.

Nor made a mental note to rescue the fish trapped in

the pond and realized that the beehive, the one that had sat along the side of the yard since the days of Rona Blackburn, was oddly quiet. Nor suspected the bees inside had drowned.

"Everyone's looking for you," Reed said, coming up behind her on the porch. He wrapped his arms around her waist and pulled her against him.

A few moments before, Pike — his arm around Charlie, whose leg had been mended — and a newly healed Sena Crowe had proposed a toast in Nor's honor. They had all somberly held up their plastic cups of frothy beer or tumblers of scotch, and Nor's face had burned with embarrassment. It felt wrong getting credit for doing something she wasn't sure she should have been able to do. Plus, there was no vanquished beast, no conquered villain to display.

Nor stared down at the blackbird tattoo etched onto Reed's arm. She thought of the blood that had dripped from Gage's ears and the puckered pink scar that would forever mar Pike's face because she hadn't been able to heal him. She thought of the inexplicable light that had poured from her hands, and the way her mother had unraveled before her eyes.

Above them, two blackbirds fought over a strand of algae tangled in the branches of an apple tree. "I should get Grayson home," Reed said after a moment. He leaned down to kiss her. She raised her lips to his and wondered if he knew, like she did, that it was likely for the last time. She had to break up with him. Like it or not, whatever path she was on would continue to be a dangerous one. He deserved to be protected from her, from what might yet come.

Nor watched him leave, prepared to bite her tongue hard to keep from crying out. But though it felt like her heart had been punctured, she was startled to find she no longer felt the impulse to spill her own blood or to taste it. Even the scars on her wrists, ankles, and arms were silent.

This pain seemed content to remain where it belonged.

Inside, Nor found an idyllic scene, so contrary to the mess still left outside. In the parlor, Dauphine and Everly shared the last few pulls from the bottle of scotch. Wintersweet sat next to the fire crackling in the hearth, quietly combing burrs out of Burn's thick pelt. Gage and Reuben sat on one of the tufted Victorian couches with their muddy boots propped up on the coffee table.

"You missed some when you washed up," Apothia said, reaching over to wipe a bit of blood from Nor's cheek with the sleeve of her sweater. She motioned upstairs. "Your grandmother wants to have a look at you."

Nor climbed up to the Tower's second floor. Along the walls hung portraits of the Blackburn daughters. Nor felt their scrutiny and imagined their gazes alternating between pride, sympathy, and disappointment.

As revealing as portraits could be, there was also much

they could conceal. The color of Greta's wild red hair was lost in her black-and-white photo. In a Kodachrome snapshot, Fern looked like a nice girl without a care in the world. Nor wondered what her own portrait might hide from the innocent viewer.

She stopped into the bathroom and splashed cool water on her face. She looked in the mirror. Her hair was tangled and singed. She tried to pull her fingers through the knots, but strands broke off and fell to the floor like dried straw.

She gathered her hair — what was left of it — against the nape of her neck and began rifling through drawers until she found what she was looking for.

"Are you sure you want to chop it off, just like that?" Gage was standing in the bathroom doorway.

"Yes, I am," Nor said defiantly, then reached back and hacked through the thick ponytail with the scissors. Triumphantly, she held it up, then dropped it into the sink. She turned her head and examined her handiwork. The left side seemed to be a bit shorter than the right, but it would have to do for now. At least Judd couldn't accuse her of hiding behind her hair anymore.

"You should have asked Savvy to do it for you," Gage said. "It looks like shit."

"That's possibly the rudest thing you've ever said to me."

"Well, now I feel extra accomplished today." He took a slight bow and smiled.

Nor thought of all the injuries he'd sustained trying to

help her — the broken fingers, the burn on his arm. She thought about how he had trudged through that flooded room, had upheld his promise to get Sena Crowe and Savvy home safe. She thought about the smear of blood she had left on his neck, like a lipstick kiss, the remnants of a lovers' tryst.

"Look, about when I kissed you —" Nor started.

"You thought you were heading to your death," Gage cut in. "It was a natural reaction. It could have been worse. If I hadn't been there, you could have ended up tonguing Sena Crowe instead."

"I did *not* tongue you!" Nor insisted.

"There was some tongue."

Nor laughed. "Shut up."

Gage smiled, holding out his hand. "It didn't count. Agreed?"

"Agreed." They shook hands, and Nor was relieved that he let go first.

Across the hall, in Judd's room, Nor found her grand-mother standing at a window, smoking her rosewood pipe. The room, full of large masculine furniture and rich-colored fabrics — all dark greens and scarlet reds and chest-nut browns — had always made Nor feel particularly small. Today was no different.

Nor's grandmother led her to a worn leather couch. Nor sat down next to Antiquity. The old dog's dream of running through the forest wasn't quite as winsome as one of Bijou's dreams, but it was a pleasant one nonetheless.

"Let me get a look at you," Judd said in her gruff way. She gripped Nor's chin with her large fingers and turned Nor's head one way and then the other. She examined Nor's hands, but nothing was left to heal. Those particular wounds had stopped hurting hours ago.

"I met my father," Nor blurted out.

That caught Judd's attention. "I suspected you might. Is he still alive?"

Nor shook her head.

"That's probably for the best." Judd grunted.

"Do you think she loved him?" Nor asked. "Do you think that's what caused all of this?"

"Some hearts can't do anything with love except turn it rotten. I think that was the case with Fern. She believed she loved him, but that love was a sour thing. Who knows what might have happened if you hadn't been powerful enough to stop her."

Nor gaped. "I'm not . . ."

"I think it's about time we start talking truth, don't you? Far as I can tell, you're a very powerful witch, Nor. Though some lessons in the healing arts probably wouldn't be a bad idea."

Nor blanched. "How did you —"

"I'd had my suspicions. It was seeing that fern, lying

there like a dried-up tongue across the kitchen table, that solidified it for me. But at that point, I didn't want to say anything out of fear that—"

"That I was somehow using black magic?"

"I should have known better," Judd said. "You're the eighth Blackburn daughter, girlie. I suspect these gifts have been yours all along. I'm sorry."

Nor wasn't sure what to say. As far as she knew, the Giantess had never apologized to anyone before in her life. "What does it mean, though?" she finally asked. "If I'm not like my mother, am I like Rona?" Nor wasn't sure that comparison would be any better. She sure as hell didn't want to be Fern, but following in their matriarch's footsteps wasn't very appealing, either.

"I think it's safe to say you are something entirely your own." Judd patted Nor's back affectionately. "Now, I hate to bring up your mother again, but letting certain people know you had a hand in her demise might work in our favor."

Nor let the shock of what her grandmother was saying settle over her. "What do you mean?"

"I think a lot of people are going to be very afraid of what people like your mother—like us—can do. And fear can make people act in all kinds of terrible ways." She turned back toward the window. "For now, though, you might think about heading off to bed. You, girlie, look like you've been through hell and back."

"I have."

"It probably wouldn't be a bad idea to take a shower, too, then, would it?" There was a catch in Judd's voice this time, causing Nor's heart to leap up into her throat. Was it possible that being Fern's mother had scarred Judd just as much as being Fern's daughter had scarred Nor?

As Nor left the room, she looked back, but Judd's face was obscured by the smoke spiraling from her pipe.

Nor climbed to the third floor as fast as her tired muscles would carry her. She found Savvy curled up on her bed, a blanket wrapped around her like a shawl. Bijou was asleep on Nor's pillow.

"I like your hair," Savvy said.

Nor laughed. "Gage said it looked like shit."

"What does he know about anything? What a dick." She paused, giving Nor a guilty look. "I mean, putting aside the fact that I'm pretty sure he saved my life, numerous times in fact, and that if not for him, I wouldn't be standing here. So, I mean, as long as you don't consider that whole mess then, you know —"

"He's a dick," Nor finished.

"Such a dick."

"I'm having trouble believing it," Nor admitted cautiously. "That she's gone."

"But she is," Savvy said, then looked alarmed. "She is, right?"

"Yeah, she's gone."

"Well. Ding dong, then."

Savvy moved over, and Nor climbed onto the bed. Through the skylight, they watched an array of colors arc over the moon like a twirling skirt: Aurora Borealis. The northern lights transformed the night sky with their undulating swirls of bright blues and yellows and greens. Nor rested her head on her best friend's shoulder.

"Yeah," Nor said softly. "Ding dong."

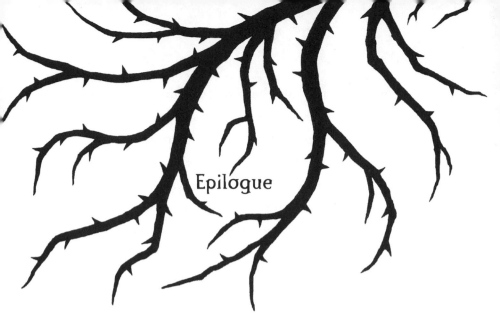

Epilogue

A late May rain slipped down Nor's bedroom windows. Her breath fogged up the glass. The blurry red-and-blue flashing lights of two police cars lit up the night. Nor glanced back at the menagerie of animals in her bedroom: Bijou and the little fox curled up together on the bed, Antiquity sitting on the floor. Kikimora perched on top of the dresser and tracking Nor's every move with golden eyes. "Stay here," she told them.

Nor found her grandmother lurking on the second-floor landing. The voices of Apothia and Reuben drifted up from the first floor, where they were greeting the officers and letting them inside. The officers' steps, resolute and unyielding, resounded loudly on the wooden floor. Their shadows crept like monsters up the winding staircase.

"What do you think they want?" Nor asked.

"You know as well as I do what they want," Judd whispered hoarsely. "They want to know what we're capable of. They want to see if we're as much of a threat as she was."

Fern's influence over her followers had ended the moment she'd died, a little over two months ago. All over the country, her millions of fans had suddenly been freed from her control, freed from that fog that had clouded their sight and their judgment. People had been stunned to learn that money hadn't been the only price paid for one of Fern Blackburn's spells. Their wishes for success, for power, for beauty had been granted, but at the cost of someone's life. Guilt-stricken, Fern's loyal followers had looked in the mirror and seen faces they didn't want to own.

A rash of suicides had followed. The waters below the Golden Gate Bridge and Niagara Falls had been littered with the bloated bodies of those who couldn't forgive themselves. The Manhattan subway stop at Union Square and Fourteenth Street had been another common spot for suicide attempts.

Anti-witch propaganda had flooded the media. Occult shops like the Witching Hour had become targets of vandalism. Schools banned the use of black nail polish. Owners of black cats kept them inside for their safety. The public was in a panic. How could they protect themselves and their families if they didn't know from what, or rather from *whom*, they needed to be protected?

"Because," as one speculative talk radio host insisted garrulously, "how likely is it that there is just *one* Fern Blackburn out there?"

In the hopes of calming a fearful nation, the president had held a press conference. In her plainspoken way, she'd reassured the public that their government would be diligent. She declared all "practitioners of conjuration" a threat to national security and urged citizens who had knowledge of someone practicing witchcraft to come forward.

Neighbor had quickly turned on neighbor. The bruja known for her homebrewed cold remedies no longer seemed so benign, nor did the local tarot reader with his eerily accurate predictions.

An organization calling themselves Families Laboring Against an Anti-Moral Environment (FLAAME) had staged a rally outside the capitol. "In Plain Sight" was their battle cry. Copies of the *Malleus Maleficarum*, a guidebook for witch hunters, had sold out in bookstores across the nation. It would have been funny if so many people hadn't taken the 1486 text so seriously.

Truthfully, Nor had known it was only a matter of time before they targeted her and her grandmother. She just hadn't thought it would happen this soon.

"What if we just deny that we're witches?" Nor asked Judd. "Insist that it's mere speculation?"

"Blackburn women have never been very good at covering their tracks," Judd answered frankly. "It's too late for us to start now. No, we're going to cooperate. We'll go with them willingly, we'll answer their questions, and hopefully, once they see we're not a threat, they'll leave us alone. Just remember, girlie," she said, peering down at Nor, "this is not the time to be stupid. Don't go showing them something they'll want to see."

A few hours later, Nor was led through a sterile police station. The reek of disinfectant — a sickly sweet orange — turned Nor's stomach. The officer she was following had seemed a lot nicer when he'd helped her into his car. Well, maybe nice wasn't exactly the word. Maybe *placid* was better.

Officer Placid left Nor in a room, shutting the door behind him with an obstinate click. The room was bleak at best. There was a table and a hard metal chair that screeched against the concrete floor when she pulled it out to sit down. On one side, a window looked out into the hall, the blinds twisted and broken, the glass smeared with fingerprints and what looked like dried blood. On the other side, a window looked out into the street where the wind continued to blow and rain beat down on cars and pedestrians.

Why was it that disaster never arrived in the middle of the day, when the noonday sun was casting prisms across the kitchen floor? Why was it always dark — and raining?

Nor tried to hold on to what Judd had told her about not

giving them anything worth seeing. *Try to be unmemorable,* Nor thought. *Check.* At least she'd had plenty of practice with that.

Officer Placid returned, carrying two additional metal chairs. He set them down on the opposite side of the table and settled heavily into one of them.

A woman in a crisp white suit and kitten heels came in next. She hesitated a moment before perching primly on the other chair, making sure to point herself away from the officer beside her. Nor didn't exactly blame her. She could smell the officer's unwashed hair and coffee breath from across the table.

Finally, a third person entered, so quietly that had he not been the one to shut the door, Nor wasn't certain she would have noticed his entrance. His otherwise handsome face was scarred with pockmarks. Standing off to the side, he smiled at her with teeth so white they were practically blue.

The woman pulled a Kleenex from her pocket and held it to her nose as she examined the tablet in her hand, flicking her fingers across the screen in quick movements. The screen radiated an electric violet across her sharp features. "Let's see then," she mused. "Nor Blackburn? Born in 1998 on the thirty-first of October, which makes you —"

Officer Placid narrowed his eyes. "A Halloween baby."

Superstitious piece of — Nor thought sourly. "It makes me seventeen," she interjected.

The woman pursed her lips in irritation. "Yes. What

I was about to say is that you are not yet legally an adult. However, in a few short months, you will be." She clucked her tongue. "Incidentally, that also means you can be charged as an adult."

"And what would I be charged with?"

"Nothing yet. Still, best to behave yourself, Miss Blackburn." The woman consulted the screen again. "Let's see. Daughter of Fern Blackburn and Quinn Sweeney, both deceased. Is that correct?"

Nor nodded, unable to forget the look on her father's face as he sank beneath the water, or the gruesome image of her mother disintegrating before her eyes. Nor swallowed hard.

"Miss Blackburn, do you understand the purpose of your visit today?" the woman asked.

Visit? Is that what this is? Nor thought. "Uh, I'm guessing you want to know if I'm a witch." She paused. "Like my mother."

The woman blinked at Nor furiously. "We already know you're a witch," she said, practically hissing. The word was a foul thing in her mouth that she had to spit out. "What we are interested in learning is if your — abilities pose a threat to the safety and security of others, like your mother's did."

"All I can do is tell you when it's going to stop raining." Nor shrugged as sheepishly as she could. "Which should be soon."

"So you can predict the weather?" The woman set the tablet down and folded her hands demurely. "How marvelous," she said flatly.

Outside, sheets of rain pounded against the windowpane as an onslaught of storm clouds, dark and ominous, rolled across the sky. "It's been raining like this for almost a week straight," the officer scoffed. "It doesn't look to me like it's letting up anytime soon."

The woman ignored the officer. "Miss Blackburn, can you be more specific? What exactly do you mean by 'soon'?"

"I mean it's already stopped."

A look out the window confirmed what had seemed impossible only a moment earlier. The sky was clear, and the setting sun was blooming like fire across the darkening sky.

"What the —" sputtered the officer.

"Is there anything else you can predict? Droughts? Earthquakes?" The man standing in the corner spoke for the first time. He was looking at Nor with interest, his blue-white teeth flashing at her like the Cheshire cat. *Shit.*

Nor shook her head. "Only rain," she answered, making up her responses as she went. "And I'm wrong most of the time."

"You weren't wrong this time." There was something particularly hungry about the way he was looking at her.

Nor gulped. "I got lucky." She'd seen this look before: a hungry, greedy look, like the face of one with an unquenchable thirst.

"That's not luck," grumbled Officer Placid. "It's unnatural, is what it is."

The man in the corner came closer. "What's your radius? Could you, for example, predict a tsunami in the Philippines?"

Nor paused. "Not unless I was in the Philippines," she finally said.

"So to be clear," the woman interrupted. "You can predict the weather. Can you, in any way, *control* the weather?"

"Oh, no," Nor said, shaking her head. "I can just tell you when it's going to rain or stop raining, which isn't much of a party trick around here." The officer did not look convinced. "My mother always considered me a great failure," she added seriously.

"Well, that's good news for us," the woman said humorlessly. "And for you." She shared a look with Officer Placid.

"It's like I said," Nor added as meekly as possible. "I'm wrong most of the time."

The man in the corner stared at her for a long minute before turning his attention back to the window. The rain had begun to fall again.

Judd was waiting for Nor outside under the awning of the police station entrance. The rain made satisfying plopping noises on the canvas. Someone's lost umbrella sat in a puddle near her feet.

Her grandmother's face remained as stoic as ever, but

Nor caught a slight tremor in her hand when she pulled out her rosewood pipe.

"What happened?" Nor murmured.

"They heard I was a healer," Judd said. "Seems they learned that from a few of our neighbors."

Nor's mouth dropped open in shock. All those people Judd had helped — how could they betray her like that? And so easily? "What did you do?"

"Not much else I could do," Judd finally answered. "I healed a woman's headache."

The rain blew over Judd's face, pooling in the deep purple bags under her eyes and the crevices etched along the sides of her mouth. She looked — old. Why did that scare Nor more than anything else that had happened that day? Even more than whatever it was that woman had been typing on that tablet of hers? Even more than the Cheshire-cat man?

"And?" Nor held her breath, praying that the pain hadn't come out as something alarming.

Judd rubbed her temples. "Rose petals."

Nor let out a sigh of relief. "It could have been worse."

It took Judd a long time to respond. "I hate to say it," she finally said, "but I think we'd better prepare ourselves for when it does get worse."

"What do you mean?" Nor asked.

"There are a lot of scared people out there right now, girlie," Judd said quietly. "And it's my opinion that nothing good has ever come of actions driven by fear."

Judd lumbered out into the rain toward Reuben's truck, which was waiting for them across the street. Nor moved to follow, but paused to pick up the broken and discarded umbrella. She absentmindedly ran a hand over it, repairing it instantly. Someone could find use for it in all this rain. She was looking for a place to leave it when she sensed movement in one of the windows behind her. The hair on the back of her neck prickled. Someone was watching her. Nor dropped the umbrella and darted out from under the awning. Not until she was safe in Reuben's warm truck did Nor dare to look back.

Grinning at her from behind the glass was the man with the Cheshire-cat smile.

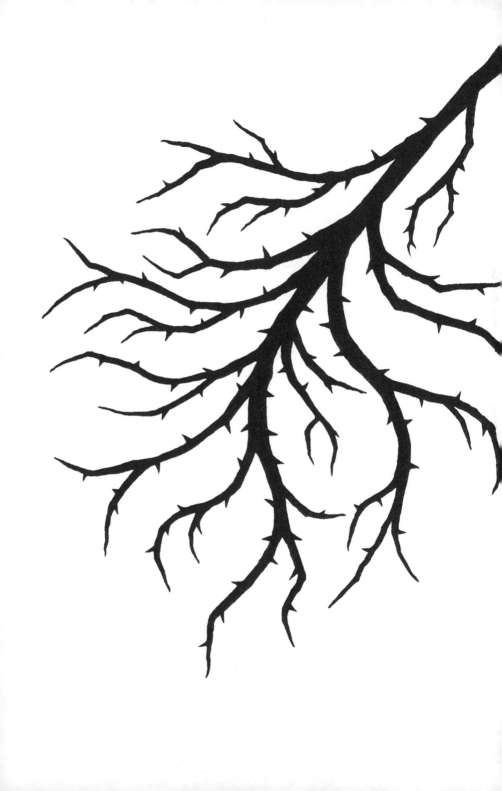

ACKNOWLEDGMENTS

First and foremost, this book would have been nothing worth reading if not for the tireless dedication, effort, and candor of my dear editor, Mary Lee Donovan. This book was a feral beast at times, and without you, Mary Lee, I would never have tamed it.

To my literary agent, Bernadette Baker-Baughman, for the enthusiasm you've always shown these strange little books and characters of mine. I am forever grateful that you've agreed to continue this journey with me. Also, many thanks to Victoria Sanders for all of your support, and Chandler Crawford for all the groundwork you laid with *The Strange and Beautiful Sorrows of Ava Lavender.* Thank you, Jessica Spivey, for all of the work you do behind the scenes, and Gretchen Stelter for starting it all!

I also owe an immense thank-you to the teams at Candlewick Press and Walker Books who have always treated me so well. Thank you for being oh, so good at what you do.

Writing can be a very solitary occupation, and I would be remiss not to thank the lovely creatures whose excitement and encouragement throughout this process have never faltered. Thank you to my fellow writers Lish McBride and Martha Brockenbrough, who are both so much more talented than I am. Thank you, Reba, Tiff, and Megan, all of whom I could always count on for a night of cocktails and conversation when I needed it most. Also thank you to Andrea, Annelise, Carissa, Duffy, Maren, Raquel, and Stephanie, whose goodness and beauty and light have surely found their way onto these pages. And thank you, Anna, for playing such an important role in the creation of this book and these characters from beginning to end. I am so glad we decided to be friends instead of enemies (because really, it could have gone either way).

Thank you to my family — Mom, Dad, Nichele, Kollin, and Kaeloni — who believe in me far more than I believe in myself. Thank you to Joe, whose love for me should serve as proof of his endless bravery and kindness. I love you and I like you. Can you thank your dog? I'm thanking my dog. Thank you to my constant companion, Mr. Darcy, the oldest, most curmudgeonly Chihuahua on the planet.

Thank you to independent booksellers, librarians, and bloggers the world over for putting books into the hands of the readers who need them. And thank you, my lovely readers. I am so glad you are here.

Finally, I would like to sincerely thank all you brave and beautiful souls who trusted me with the stories of your struggles with self harm. Your courage inspired me to write this story. May it remind all of us that our scars, be they on the inside or the outside, are proof not of our frailty, but of our strength. They are not evidence that the dark inside of us is something to fear.

No, it is the darkness that should be afraid of *us*.

If you or a loved one is struggling with self harm, please remember you're not alone. Consider reaching out to one of these resources for help:

S.A.F.E. Alternatives (www.selfinjury.com) is a world-renowned treatment program dedicated to ending self-injurious behavior. Provides resources for families and schools, as well as a psychiatric locator. The S.A.F.E. Alternatives hotline is (800)-DONTCUT (366-8288).

Self Injury Foundation (www.selfinjuryfoundation.org) provides support, advocacy, and education for self-injurers and their families.

Self Injury Outreach and Support (www.sioutreach.org) is a nonprofit organization. Their website is filled with resources, videos, and personal stories told by people who have struggled with self harm. Self-injurers and those in recovery, as well as their loved ones, will all find resources here.

The Trevor Project (www.thetrevorproject.org/pages/self -injury-resource) is an online resource for LGBTQ teens who practice self harm.

Additional resources include:

selfharmUK: www.selfharm.co.uk

HelpGuide: www.helpguide.org/articles/anxiety/cutting
-and-self-harm.htm

The Butterfly Project: http://butterfly-project.tumblr.com

To Write Love on Her Arms: https://twloha.com

TheHopeLine: www.thehopeline.com/struggles-with-self
-harm